Christopher Marlowe's Dido, Queen of Carthage: A Retelling

David Bruce

Published by David Bruce, 2022.

CHRISTOPHER MARLOWE'S DIDO, QUEEN OF CARTHAGE: A RETELLING

First edition. July 12, 2022.

ISBN: 979-8201369606

Written by David Bruce.

Table of Contents

Cover Photo for Christopher Marlowe's *Dido, Queen of Carthage*: A Retelling

***

Cover Photo:
https://pixabay.com/en/girl-portrait-woman-sad-2961959/

Dedicated to Carl Eugene Bruce and Josephine Saturday Bruce

***

Educate Yourself

Read Like A Wolf Eats

Be Excellent to Each Other

Books Then, Books Now, Books Forever

***

In this retelling, as in all my retellings, I have tried to make the work of literature accessible to modern readers who may lack some of the knowledge about mythology, religion, and history that the literary work's contemporary audience had.

Do you know a language other than English? If you do, I give you permission to translate this book, copyright your translation, publish or self-publish it, and keep all the royalties for yourself. (Do give me credit, of course, for the original retelling.)

I would like to see my retellings of classic literature used in schools, so I give permission to the country of Finland (and all other countries) to buy (or get free) one copy of this eBook and give copies to all students forever. I also give permission to the state of Texas (and all other states) to buy (or get free) one copy of this eBook and give copies to all students forever. I also give permission to all teachers to buy (or get free) one copy of this eBook and give copies to all students forever.

Teachers need not actually teach my retellings. Teachers are welcome to give students copies of my eBooks as background material. For example, if they are teaching Homer's *Iliad* and *Odyssey*, teachers are welcome to give students copies of my *Virgil's* Aeneid: *A Retelling in Prose* and tell students, "Here's another ancient epic you may want to read in your spare time."

CAST OF CHARACTERS

Gods:

Jupiter, King of the Gods.

Mercury (Hermes), the Messenger God. Mercury is the god's Roman name, and Hermes is the god's Greek name. Christopher Marlowe uses both names in this play.

Ganymede, Cupbearer to the Gods.

Cupid, God of Love.

Goddesses:

Venus, Goddess of Love and Beauty and Sexual Passion.

Juno, Queen of the Gods.

Trojans:

Aeneas, Leader of the exiled Trojans after the Fall of Troy.

Ascanius, his son.

Achates.

Ilioneus.

Cloanthus.

Sergestus.

Aeneas' Rival:

Iarbas, King of Gaetulia.

Carthaginians:

Dido, Queen of Carthage.

Anna, her sister.

Nurse.

Minor Characters:

Trojan Soldiers, Carthaginian Lords, Attendants.

NOTE:

Thomas Nashe may be a co-author of this play.

CHAPTER 1
— 1.1 —

On Mount Olympus, Jupiter dandled Ganymede upon his knee and Mercury lay asleep.

"Come, gentle Ganymede, and play with me," Jupiter said. "I love you well, and I don't care what Juno says."

Ganymede was a beautiful young boy, and Jupiter loved him. Jupiter was unfaithful to his wife, Juno, and had many affairs with goddesses and mortal women.

"I am 'much better off' because of your worthless love," Ganymede said sarcastically, "that will not shield me from her shrewish blows. Today, when I poured nectar in your cups and held the fine napkin while you drank, she reached over and hit me so hard that I spilled the nectar, and she made the blood run down from my ears."

The gods drank nectar and ate ambrosia.

"What!" Jupiter said. "Does she dare strike the darling of my thoughts? By Saturn's soul, and this earth-threatening hair, that, shaken thrice, makes nature's buildings quake, I vow that if she just once frowns on you again, to hang her, like a meteor, between heaven and earth, and bind her, hand and foot, with golden cords, as once I did after she harmed Hercules."

Jupiter was a powerful god. To become the King of the gods, he had to overpower his father, Saturn, and just by shaking his hair three times he could cause earthquakes that would shake mountains.

Juno hated the children that Jupiter fathered with other goddesses and women. One of these children was the super-strong Hercules, whom Juno once caused to be shipwrecked. To punish Juno, Jupiter tied her with golden ropes, hung anvils from her feet, and let her hang suspended by her hands.

"If I might just see that pretty entertainment afoot," Ganymede said, "oh, how I would laugh with Helen's brother, and bring the gods to see and wonder at Juno's punishment."

Helen is Helen of Troy, and her brother would be either Castor or Pollux. They were her twin brothers, but Castor was mortal and Pollux was immortal. After Castor died, Pollux shared his immortality with him. The brothers took turns being alive: While one twin was happy and alive on Mount Olympus with the other gods, the other twin was in Hades, the Land of the Dead.

Ganymede continued, "Sweet Jupiter, if I have ever pleased your eye or seemed fair, walled in with eagle's wings, grace my immortal beauty with this favor, and I will spend my time in your bright arms."

Earlier, Jupiter had turned himself into an eagle, swooped down and seized the extremely good-looking Ganymede, and carried him to Mount Olympus to be his cupbearer. Although Ganymede had been born mortal, Jupiter gave him eternal youth.

"What would I deny your youth, you sweet boy," Jupiter said, "whose face reflects such pleasure to my eyes, as I, burning with passion on account of the fire-darting beams from your eyes, have often driven back the horses of the night, when they would have haled you from my sight?"

Jupiter was saying that he had often kept back the horses of the night, but did he keep them from rising or from setting? If he kept them from rising and beginning the night, he did so because he wanted to spend more time with Ganymede before Ganymede got sleepy and went to bed. If he kept them from setting and ending the night, he did so because he wanted to spend more time with Ganymede in bed.

Jupiter continued, "Sit on my knee and call for whatever you want. Control proud Fate and cut the thread of Time."

The three Fates determined the length of mortal lives. Clotho spun the thread of life, Lachesis measured it, and Atropos cut it. When a mortal's thread of life was cut, the mortal died.

Jupiter continued, "Why, aren't all the gods at your command and aren't heaven and earth the territory of your delight? The lame blacksmith god Vulcan shall dance to make laughing entertainment for you, and my nine daughters — the Graces — shall sing for you when you are sad. From Juno's bird the peacock I'll pluck her spotted pride — her feathers — to make you fans with which to cool your face, and Venus' swans shall shed their silver down to make sweet the slumbers of your soft bed. Hermes no more shall show the world his wings, if your fancy should dwell in his feathers, for, as I do this one, I'll tear them all from him."

Jupiter plucked a feather from one of the winged sandals or the winged cap that Hermes wore.

Jupiter continued, "Do just say, 'Their color pleases me,' and I will pluck them."

He then gave Ganymede a necklace of jewels and said, "Hold this here, my little love. These linked gems my Juno wore on her marriage day. My own sweetheart, put this around your neck and decorate your arms and shoulders with my theft."

"I also want a jewel for my ear and a fine brooch to put in my hat," Ganymede said, "and then I'll hug with you a hundred times."

"And you shall have those things, Ganymede, if you will be my love."

Venus entered and complained, "Yes, this is it! You can sit toying there and playing with that effeminate wanton boy, while my son Aeneas — a mortal — wanders on the seas and remains a prey to every ocean wave's pride. He is in danger of being shipwrecked."

Aeneas had become the leader of the surviving free Trojans after the fall of Troy. They had built 24 ships and were sailing in search of a new homeland.

Venus continued, "Juno, false and treacherous Juno, in her chariot's pomp, drawn through the heavens by steeds of the brood of Boreas, the North Wind, ordered the goddess Hebe to direct the airy wheels of Juno's chariot to the windy country of the clouds, where, finding Aeolus, guardian of the winds, entrenched with storms and guarded by a thousand grisly ghosts, she humbly begged him to be our bane, and told him to drown my son with all his fellow Trojans."

Aeolus kept the winds locked up, releasing only the winds he wanted to be released for a while. If Aeolus kept the storm winds locked up, then ships could sail safely, but if he released the storm winds, then ships could sink.

Venus continued, "Then began the winds to break open their brazen doors and all Aeolia — Aeolus' islands — to be up in arms.

"Poor Troy must now be sacked upon the sea, and Neptune's waves be malicious men of war. Epeus' horse, transformed to Mount Etna's volcanic hill, stands prepared to wrack their wooden walls, and Aeolus, like Agamemnon, sounds the surges, his fierce soldiers, to the spoil."

Venus was comparing the danger of the storm to the fall of Troy. Aeneas' ships were Troy, and they were in danger of sinking. Epeus had built the Trojan Horse, which the Trojans had brought into their city, widening the entrance into the city to do so. The rocks around the island of Mount Etna would similarly poke holes in Aeneas' ships. Agamemnon had led the Greek warriors in the war against Troy.

Venus continued, "See how the night, Ulysses-like, comes forth and intercepts the day, as Ulysses formerly intercepted Dolon."

The storm clouds were making everything dark, and so night was surprising day. In Book 10 of Homer's *Iliad*, Odysseus (his Roman name is Ulysses) and Diomedes make a night raid and surprise and capture Dolon, a Trojan spy.

Venus said, "Ay me! The stars surprised, like Rhesus' steeds, are drawn by darkness from the tents of Astraeus, a Titan and the father of the stars."

"Ay me" is an expression of grief.

Because the storm clouds were making everything dark, the stars came out early, although they could not be seen because of the storm clouds. They were surprised, just like the steeds of King Rhesus were surprised. After capturing Dolon, Ulysses and Diomedes extracted information from him, learning that a King named Rhesus had recently arrived. Ulysses and Diomedes killed King Rhesus and stole his horses. No one saw Ulysses and Diomedes killing the King and stealing his horses.

Venus continued, "What shall I do to save you, Aeneas, my sweet boy, when the waves are so high that they threaten our divine crystalline world above the clouds, and the sea-god Proteus, raising hills of floods on high, intends before long to entertain himself in the sky?

"False, treacherous Jupiter, is this how you reward virtue? What! Isn't piety exempt from woe? My son Aeneas is a pious man. But if you, Jupiter, reward his piety in this way, then die, Aeneas, in your innocence, since your religion and piety receive no recompense."

She believed that her son deserved much better treatment than this because of his good personal character.

Jupiter said, "Be calm, Cytherea, despite your concern for your son."

One of Venus' names was Cytherea because she was born in the sea near the island of Cythera.

Jupiter continued, "Your Aeneas' wandering fate is firm and fixed; we know what is fated to happen to him, both as he wanders and afterward."

He now described Aeneas' fate:

"His weary limbs shall shortly find repose in those fair walls I previously promised him. But his good fortune must first bud in blood before he becomes the lord of the town of Turnus, or force Juno to smile although she has hitherto frowned. Three winters shall he with the Rutulians war, and in the end subdue them with his sword, and three full summers likewise shall he waste in taming those fierce barbarian minds. Once that is performed, then poor Troy, so long suppressed, from out of her ashes shall advance her strength and power, and the Trojans shall flourish once again, although they were 'dead' just after the fall of Troy."

As a god, Jupiter knew Aeneas' fate. Eventually, he would lead the free surviving Trojans to Italy, where they would fight a war for three years. Eventually, the Trojans would win the war, with Aeneas killing Turnus, the leader of the enemy forces. Then the Trojans would become important ancestors of the Roman people. Although Juno hated the Trojans, she would be forced to accept their success.

Jupiter continued to tell Aeneas' fate:

"But bright Ascanius, beauty's better work, who with the sun divides one radiant shape, shall build his throne in the midst of those starry towers that earth-born Atlas, groaning, underprops and supports."

Ascanius is Aeneas' son, beautiful and as radiant as the sun. Atlas is a Titan who was punished by being forced to hold up the sky.

Jupiter continued to tell Aeneas' fate, including the fate of his descendants:

"No boundaries but heaven shall bound his empire, whose azured — blue-as-the-sky — gates engraved with his name, shall make the morning hasten her gray uprise to feed her eyes with his engraved fame."

The Roman Empire would have no boundary except that of heaven, and Aeneas' name and the names of his important descendants would be remembered.

Jupiter continued to tell Aeneas' fate, including the fate of his descendants:

"Thus in brave Hector's race the Roman royal scepter shall remain for three hundred years, until a priestess of royal birth impregnated by Mars, shall yield to dignity a double birth, who will make Troy eternal with their undertakings."

Hector was the greatest Trojan warrior, but the greatest warrior of the Trojan War, the Greek Achilles, killed him.

Aeneas and his descendants were fated to build and rule cities in Italy. Three hundred years after Aeneas, the vestal virgin Rhea Silvia, also known as Ilia, would give birth to the twins Romulus and Remus, who would found the city of Rome.

Venus said, "How may I believe these flattering words of yours, when both sea and sands still beset the Trojan ships, and Phoebus Apollo refrains from tainting his tresses in the Tyrrhenian main just as he refrains from tainting them in Stygian pools?"

She was saying in a complex way what could be said simply. Phoebus Apollo is the sun-god, and in this case he is metaphorically the sun itself. "Tainting his tresses" meant "dipping his hair" or "shining on." The Tyrrhenian main is the Mediterranean Sea. The Styx is a river in Hades, the Land of the Dead. All that Venus was saying was that the sun was refraining from shining on the Mediterranean Sea just like it refrained from shining on the Styx River in the underground Land of the Dead.

"I will take care of that immediately," Jupiter said to Venus.

He shook Hermes and said, "Hermes, wake up, and hasten to the realm of Neptune, King of the sea, where the wind god, Aeolus, warring now with Fate, is besieging the offspring of our kingly loins.

"Order him from me to turn his stormy powers back to his realm and fetter them in Vulcan's sturdy brass restraints because these stormy winds dare to thus proudly wrong our kinsman's peace."

Aeneas was a kinsman because he could trace his ancestry back to Jupiter, who with Electra parented Dardanus, from whom Aeneas was descended.

Hermes exited to carry out his orders.

"Venus, farewell," Jupiter said. "I will take care of your son Aeneas."

He then said, "Come, Ganymede, we must set about this business."

Jupiter and Ganymede exited.

Gods and goddesses can move quickly. Venus quickly flew through the air and landed on the shore of Carthage, where she knew that Aeneas would soon appear.

She said, "Restless seas, lay down your swelling looks, and court Aeneas with your calm cheer, whose beauteous burden well might make you proud, had not the heavens, made pregnant with hell-born clouds, veiled his resplendent glory from your view.

"For my sake pity him, Oceanus, you river that encircles the world. Pity Aeneas for the sake of me, who formerly issued from watery loins and had my being from your bubbling froth. I was born from the foam around the island of Cythera.

"The sea-god Triton, I know, has blown his trumpet on behalf of Troy, and therefore will take pity on Aeneas' toil, and call both Thetis and Cymothoe, two Nereids who are minor sea-goddesses, to succor him in this extremity."

When Triton blows his trumpet, waves calm. Venus must have thought — or known — that Jupiter had ordered him to calm the waves.

Aeneas arrived, accompanied by Ascanius and one or two other Trojans. Ascanius was Aeneas' young son, and Aeneas was Venus' adult son.

Venus said, "Do I see my son now come on shore? Venus, how you are enveloped with happiness while your eyes bring to you the joys your eyes have long sought!

"Great Jupiter, may you be always honored for this so friendly aid in time of need.

"Here in these bushes I will stand disguised as a mortal, while my Aeneas wearies himself in complaints and lets heaven and earth know about his disquiet."

Aeneas said, "You sons of care, companions of my course, Priam's misfortune follows us by sea, and Helen's abduction haunts you at the heels."

King Priam died when Troy fell. The cause of the war was his son Paris' visit to Sparta, where he seized and ran away with Helen, the legitimate wife of Menelaus, King of Sparta.

"How many dangers have we passed through and endured!" Aeneas said. "Both barking Scylla and the sounding rocks, the Cyclopes' sandbanks, and grim Ceraunia's seat have you passed and yet remain alive!"

Scylla was a monster that lived in a rocky cliffside; she would snatch sailors from ships and devour them. The sounding rocks were rocks that crashed together, smashing to bits any ships that sailed in between them. The Cyclopes were one-eyed giants that ate humans. Ceraunia was a dangerous promontory.

"Pluck up your hearts," Aeneas continued, "since fate still remains our friend, and changing heavens may return to us those good days, which Pergama did boast in all her pride."

Pergama is another name for the citadel, aka fortress, of Troy.

Achates, one of Aeneas' companions, said, "Brave Prince of Troy, you are our only god. By your virtues you free us from troubles and make our hopes survive to coming joys. If you just smile, the cloudy heaven will clear; the sky's night and day descend from your brows. Although we are now in extreme misery and remain the picture of weather-beaten woe, yet the aged sun shall shed forth his hair — his blazing tresses — to make us live with our former heat, and every beast the forest shall send forth shall bequeath her young ones to augment our scanty food."

Ascanius, hungry, said, "Father, I am faint. Good father, give me food."

"Alas, sweet boy," Aeneas said, "you must be hungry a while longer, until we have fire to cook the meat we killed.

"Gentle Achates, get the tinderbox, so that we may make a fire to warm us and roast our newfound food on this shore."

Still unnoticed, Venus said to herself, "See what strange arts necessity finds out: Necessity is the mother of invention. To what troubles, my sweet Aeneas, have you been driven!"

"Wait, take this candle and go light a fire," Aeneas said. "You shall have leaves and wind-fallen boughs enough, near to these woods, to roast your meat with.

"Ascanius, go and dry your drenched limbs, while I with my Achates rove abroad, to learn what coast the wind has driven us on, and whether men or beasts inhabit it."

Ascanius and the Trojan men exited, leaving behind Aeneas, Achates, and Venus.

"The air is pleasant," Achates said, "and the soil is most fit for the support of cities and society. Yet I much marvel that I cannot find any steps of men imprinted in the earth."

Venus said to herself, "Now is the time for me to play my part."

Disguised as a young woman, she called, "Ho, young men! Did you see as you came any of my sisters wandering here? Each sister would be wearing a quiver tied around her side and would be clothed in a spotted leopard's skin."

"I neither saw nor heard of any such," Aeneas said. "But what may I, fair virgin, call your name, you whose looks set forth no mortal form to view, and whose speech does not betray anything human in your birth?

"You are a goddess who is deluding our eyes and you are shrouding your beauty in this borrowed shape, but whether you are the sun's bright sister — Diana, twin sister of Apollo — or you are one of chaste Diana's attendant nymphs, live happy in the height of all content, and lighten our extremes with this one boon. Please tell us under what good heaven we breathe now, and what this world is called on which we are cast by the fury of the tempest.

"Tell us, oh, tell us, tell us who are ignorant, and this right hand shall make your altars crack with mountain heaps of milk-white sacrifice."

Although Venus had disguised herself as a mortal, she was unable to hide all her beauty and so Aeneas knew that she was a goddess. He was asking her for information with the promise that he would reward her by sacrificing many milk-white — the most prized color — animals on her altars.

Still pretending to be mortal, the disguised Venus said, "Such honor, stranger, I do not care for. It is the custom for Tyrian maidens to wear their bow and quiver in this modest way and clothe themselves in these purple garments so that they may travel more lightly over the meadows, and overtake the tusked boar in chase."

Venus was pretending to be a Carthaginian. The Carthaginians had come from Phoenicia, two of whose main cities were Tyre and Sidon. The Phoenicians were famous, among other things, for dyeing cloth purple.

The disguised Venus continued, "But as for the land about which you inquire, it is the Punic kingdom, rich and strong, adjoining on Agenor's stately town, the kingly seat of southern Libya, where Sidonian — Phoenician — Dido rules as Queen."

In other words, Aeneas had landed on the shore of the Punic — Carthaginian — kingdom, which was ruled by Queen Dido.

"But who are you who ask me these things?" the disguised Venus asked. "Whence may you come, or whither will you go? Where have you come from, and to where are you going?"

"I am Trojan. Aeneas is my name, who driven by war from my native world, put sails to sea to seek out Italy; I am divinely descended from sceptered Jove."

Jove is another name for Jupiter. As King of the gods, he had a scepter.

Aeneas continued, "With twice twelve ships from Asia Minor, I plowed the deep sea and headed in the direction my mother, Venus, led, but of them all scarcely seven ships anchor safely here, and they are so ravaged and rolled by the waves that every tide makes them tilt on one or other of their oaken sides.

"And all of them, unburdened of their load, are ballasted with billows' watery weight — they are filled with unwanted water.

"But hapless I, God knows, poor and unknown, do walk these Libyan deserts all despised, exiled from both Europe and wide Asia, and I haven't any roof over me except heaven."

"Fortune has favored you, whoever you are," the disguised Venus said, "in sending you to this courteous coast. In God's name, continue on, and hasten to the court, where Queen Dido will receive you with her smiles.

"And as for your other ships, which you suppose to be lost, not one of them has perished in the storm, for they have arrived safely not far from here.

"And so I leave you to your fortune's lot, wishing good luck to your wandering steps."

Venus, Aeneas' mother, quickly exited. Mortals and immortals are quite different, and it is unusual for mortal children to communicate in any depth with immortal parents.

Aeneas said, "Achates, it is my mother who has just fled; I know her by the gait of her feet.

"Wait, gentle Venus! Don't flee from your son! Too cruel, why will you forsake me thus, or in these disguises deceive my eyes so often?

"Why can't we talk together, hand in hand, and tell our griefs in more familiar terms? But you have gone and left me here alone to dull the air with my disgruntled moans."

The Trojans Cloanthus, Ilioneus, and Sergestus had just entered Carthage, where they saw Iarbas, King of Gaetulia. These Trojans were some of those who had been separated from Aeneas.

Ilioneus said, "Follow, you Trojans, follow this brave lord, and complain and explain to him the sum of your distress."

"Why, who are you, and for what do you plead?" Iarbas asked.

"We are wretches of Troy, hated by all the winds," Ilioneus replied. "We crave such favor at your honor's feet, as poor distressed misery may plead."

The Trojans knelt before Iarbas.

Ilioneus pleaded, "Save, save, oh, save our ships from cruel fire, ships that complain about the wounds of a thousand waves, and spare the lives of us whom every vexation pursues. We come not, we, to wrong your Libyan gods or steal your household Lares from their shrines."

The Lares were household gods that protected the welfare of families.

Ilioneus continued, "Our hands are not prepared to lawlessly spoil and plunder, nor are our hands armed to offend in any way. Such force is far from our unweaponed — unarmed — thoughts, whose fading well-being, lacking victory, forbids all hope to harbor near our hearts."

"But tell me, Trojans, if you are Trojans," Iarbas said, "to what fruitful quarters were you bound before Boreas — the North Wind — battled with your sails?"

"There is a place, called Hesperia by us," Cloanthus said. "It is an ancient empire, famous for arms, and fertile in fair Ceres' furrowed wealth. That place now we call Italia, of his name who in such peace for a long time and long ago did rule the same."

Hesperia — the Western Land — is an ancient name for Italy, which according to legend was ruled at one time by a King named Italia.

Cloanthus continued, "Thither made we, when suddenly gloomy Orion rose and led our ships into the shallow sands, where the southern wind with brackish breath dispersed them all amongst the wreck-causing rocks."

The constellation Orion is associated with storms.

He continued, "From thence a few of us escaped to land. The rest, we fear, are enfolded in the floods and drowned."

"Brave men-at-arms," Iarbas said, "abandon fruitless fears because Carthage knows how to courteously treat distressed men."

"Yes," Sergestus said, "but the barbarous sort of people threaten our ships and will not let us lodge upon the sands. In multitudes they swarm to the shore and they keep our feet from land."

"I myself will see to it that they shall not trouble you," Iarbas said. "Your men and you shall banquet in our court, and every Trojan will be as welcome here as Jupiter to good Baucis' house."

The gods Jupiter and Mercury once traveled in disguise as poor peasants in order to test the hospitality of people. Most people did not give them hospitality, but married couple Baucis and Philemon did, sharing what food they had although they were an unsophisticated country couple.

Iarbas continued, "Come in with me. I'll bring you to my Queen, Dido, who shall confirm my words with further deeds."

The Trojans stood up.

"Thanks, gentle lord, for such unlooked-for grace," Sergestus replied. "If we could but once more see Aeneas' face, then we would hope to reward such friendly turns as shall surpass the wonder of our speech. We aren't able to describe well enough the good you do for us."

CHAPTER 2

— 2.1 —

Aeneas, Achates, and Ascanius stood in front of a wall of a stone building in Carthage. The wall was decorated with bas-relief sculpture. The sculpture depicted the city of Troy, including its walls.

"Where am I now?" Aeneas said, looking at the depiction of Trojan walls. "These should be the walls of Carthage."

"Why stands my sweet Aeneas thus amazed?" Achates asked.

"Oh, my Achates," Aeneas said, "Theban Niobe, who for her sons' deaths wept out life and breath and, dry with grief, was turned into a stone, had not such passions in her head as I."

The mortal Niobe had several sons and several daughters, causing her to be proud and consider herself worthy of more respect than the goddess Latona, who had given birth to only one son and one daughter: Apollo and Diana. Unfortunately for Niobe, Apollo and Diana killed all of her sons and daughters.

Aeneas continued, pointing at various places in the bas-relief, "I think that town there should be Troy. Yonder is Mount Ida. There is the Xanthus' stream. I know these things because here is Priam, King of Troy. But when I know it is not Troy, because Troy has been destroyed, then I die inside."

Achates replied, "And sharing in this mood of yours is Achates, too. I cannot choose but fall upon my knees and kiss the hand of this bas-relief of King Priam."

He kissed Priam's hand and then continued, "Oh, where is Queen Hecuba?"

He pointed to the place beside King Priam and said, "Here she was accustomed to sit, but, except for air, there is nothing here. And what is this but stone?"

Aeneas said, "Yet this stone makes Aeneas weep! And I wish that my prayers (as Pygmalion's did) could give this bas-relief of King Priam life so that under his command we might sail back to Troy and be revenged on these hardhearted Grecians who rejoice that nothing now is left of King Priam."

Pygmalion was a sculptor who sculpted a perfect woman, with whom he fell in love. He prayed to the gods to make the sculpture live and the gods granted his request.

Aeneas engaged in wishful thinking, wishing that Priam were still alive and the Trojans could board ships and return home and get revenge on those who had conquered Troy: "Oh, Priam still exists, and this is he! Come, come aboard; pursue the hateful Greeks."

"What does Aeneas mean?" Achates asked.

Aeneas replied, "Achates, though my eyes say this is stone, yet my mind thinks that this is Priam, and when my grieving heart sighs and says no, then it would leap out to give Priam life. Oh, I wish I were not alive at all, as long as you — Priam — might be alive! I would gladly lose my life in order to give you life.

"Achates, look! King Priam waves his hand! He is alive! Troy is not overcome and conquered!"

Achates replied, "Your mind, Aeneas, that wishes what you say were true, deludes your eyesight. Priam is indeed dead."

Weeping, Aeneas said, "Ah, Troy has been sacked and Priam is dead, and why then should poor Aeneas be alive?"

"Sweet father, stop weeping," Ascanius said. "This is not Priam, for if it were Priam, he would smile on me."

Achates said, "Aeneas, look. Here come the citizens. Stop lamenting, lest they laugh at our fears."

Cloanthus, Ilioneus, Sergestus, and others arrived.

The Trojans did not recognize each other. Cloanthus, Ilioneus, and Sergestus were now wearing rich Carthaginian clothing, while Aeneas,

Achates, and Ascanius were wearing ragged, travel-stained clothing. The storm had been rough on their clothing.

Aeneas said, "Lords of this town, or whatsoever title belong to your names, out of compassion for us please tell us who inhabits this fair town, what kind of people and who governs them, for we are strangers driven on this shore and we scarcely know within what territory we are."

"I hear Aeneas' voice," Ilioneus said, "but I don't see him, for none of these men can be our general."

"This noble man speaks and sounds like Ilioneus, but Ilioneus doesn't wear such robes," Achates said.

"You are Achates, or I am deceived," Sergestus said.

"Aeneas, see Sergestus or his ghost!" Achates said.

"He says the name of Aeneas," Ilioneus said. "Let us kiss his feet."

"It is our captain!" Cloanthus said. "See Ascanius!"

"Live long Aeneas and Ascanius!" Sergestus said.

"Achates, speak, for I am overjoyed," Aeneas said.

"Oh, Ilioneus, are you still alive?" Achates asked.

"Blest be the time I see Achates' face," Ilioneus replied.

Overcome with emotion, Aeneas turned aside.

"Why does Aeneas turn away from his trusty friends?" Cloanthus asked.

"Sergestus, Ilioneus, and the rest," Aeneas said, "your sight amazed me. Oh, what destinies have brought my sweet companions in so good a situation? Oh, tell me, for I long to know."

"Lovely Aeneas, these are the walls of Carthage," Ilioneus said, "and here Queen Dido wears the imperial crown. She for Troy's sake has entertained us all and clad us in these wealthy robes we wear. Often has she asked us under whom we served, and when we told her, she would weep for grief, thinking the sea had swallowed up your ships.

"And now when she sees you, how she will rejoice!"

Cloanthus, Sergestus, and Ilioneus led Aeneas and the others into the building, which was Queen Dido's palace.

Sergestus pointed and said, "See where her servants are passing through the hall, bearing a banquet. Dido is not far away."

"Look where she comes!" Ilioneus said. "Aeneas, view her well."

"Well may I view her, but she does not see me," Aeneas replied.

Dido and her retinue walked over to the Trojans. Anna, her sister, was with her.

Aeneas was wrong: Dido did notice him and asked, "What stranger are you who eye me thus?"

"Formerly I was a Trojan, mighty Queen, but Troy no longer exists," Aeneas replied. "Who then shall I say I am?"

"Renowned Dido," Ilioneus said. "He is our general and leader: warlike Aeneas."

"Warlike Aeneas, and in these lowly and base robes!" Dido said.

Due to travel, travail, and the recent storm, Aeneas' clothing was ragged.

Dido ordered an attendant, "Go fetch the garment that Sichaeus wore."

Sichaeus was her late husband.

The attendant exited and quickly brought back the robe, which Aeneas put on.

"Brave Prince, welcome to Carthage and to me, both happy that Aeneas is our guest," Dido said. "Sit in this chair and banquet with a Queen. Aeneas is Aeneas, even if he were clad in clothing as bad and ragged as ever Irus wore."

Irus was a beggar who appears in Homer's *Odyssey*. He begged from and ran errands for the young men who were courting Odysseus' wife, Penelope. Odysseus' Roman name is Ulysses.

"This is no seat for one who's comfortless," Aeneas said. "May it please your grace to let Aeneas wait on you and serve you food, for although my birth is great, my fortune is mean — too mean to be companion to a Queen."

"Your fortune may be greater than your birth," Dido said. "Sit down, Aeneas, sit in Dido's place, and if this is your son, as I suppose he is, let him sit here."

She sat Ascanius on her lap and said, "Be merry, lovely child."

"This place is not suitable for me," Aeneas said. "It is too grand, pardon me."

Aeneas' humility irritated Dido, who said, "I'll have it so. Aeneas, be content and don't complain."

Aeneas sat next to Dido.

"Madam, you shall be my mother," Ascanius said.

His mother had died during the fall of Troy.

"And so I will, sweet child," Dido said.

She then said to Aeneas, "Be merry, man! Here's to your better fortune and good stars."

"In all humility, I thank your grace," Aeneas said.

"Remember who you are," Dido said. "Speak like yourself. Humility belongs to common servants."

Aeneas asked, "And who is as miserable as Aeneas is?"

"It lies in Dido's hands to make you blest, so then be assured that you are not miserable."

"Oh, Priam! Oh, Troy! Oh, Hecuba!" Aeneas said, mourning.

"May I ask and persuade you to discourse at large, and truly, too, about how Troy was overcome?" Dido asked. "Many tales are told of that city's fall, and scarcely do they agree upon one point. Some say the Trojan Antenor betrayed the town. Others report that it was Sinon's perjury that led to Troy's fall. But all stories agree that Troy is conquered and Priam is dead. Yet how that happened, we hear no certain news."

"A woeful tale Dido asks me to unfold," Aeneas said, "whose memory, like pale Death's stony mace, beats forth my senses from this troubled soul and makes Aeneas sink at Dido's feet."

"Does Aeneas faint to remember Troy, in whose defense he fought so valiantly?" Dido said. "Look up and speak."

Aeneas replied, "Then speak, Aeneas, with Achilles' tongue, and Dido and you Carthaginian peers hear me, but do so with the Myrmidons' harsh ears, which were daily inured to broils and massacres, lest you be moved too much with my sad tale."

Achilles and the warriors he led — the Myrmidons — were strong and tough and used to bloodshed, of which Aeneas' story would include much.

Aeneas began his story:

"The Grecian soldiers, tired with ten years' war, began to cry, 'Let us go to our ships! Troy is invincible. Why do we stay here?'

"Atrides — Agamemnon, leader of the Greek soldiers — being appalled by their cries, summoned the Greek captains to his princely tent. Then the captains, looking on the scars we Trojans gave, and seeing the number of their men decreased and the remainder weak and out of heart, cried out their votes to dislodge the camp.

"And so all marched in troops to Tenedos, where when they came, Ulysses on the sand attempted with honey words to turn them back."

Tenedos is an island. The Greek soldiers marched to the shore, from where they could see the island.

Aeneas continued:

"And as Ulysses spoke to further his intent, the winds drove huge billows to the shore, and heaven was darkened with tempestuous clouds. Then he alleged the gods would have them stay, and he prophesied Troy would be overcome."

Ulysses claimed that the gods had sent contrary winds in order to keep the Greeks at Troy. The winds were contrary because they would not allow the Greeks to sail home.

Aeneas continued:

"For that purpose he called forth false Sinon, a man compact of craft and perjury, whose enticing tongue was made of Hermes' pipe, to force a hundred watchful eyes to sleep."

Hermes once played his musical pipe — a flute — to lull Argos, who had a hundred eyes, to sleep.

Aeneas continued:

"And once Epeus had made the horse, Ulysses sent lying Sinon, with sacrificing wreaths upon his head, to our unhappy town of Troy. Our Phrygian shepherds dragged Sinon, groveling in the mire of the banks of the Xanthus River, his hands bound at his back, and both his eyes turned up to heaven, like one resolved to die, within the gates of Troy and brought him to the court of Priam."

Ulysses thought up the trick of the Trojan Horse, which Epeus built. The Trojan Horse was a huge, hollow, wooden horse that Sinon told the Trojans was dedicated to Minerva. The Greeks built the Trojan Horse and left it at Troy as they pretended to sail home, but instead of returning to Greece, they sailed behind the island of Tenedos, which hid them.

The Greeks left behind Sinon, who told the Trojans that he had escaped from being made a human sacrifice by Ulysses and the other Greeks.

Aeneas continued:

"Sinon acted in such a way that he aroused pity in King Priam of Troy. Sinon looked so remorseful and made so many seemingly forthright — but actually perjured — vows that the Greeks had treated him badly that the old King, overcome by Sinon, kissed him, embraced him, and untied his bonds. And then —

"Oh, Dido, pardon me!"

Aeneas was overcome by bad memories.

Dido said, "No, don't stop telling your story! Tell me the rest!"

Aeneas continued:

"Oh, the enchanting words of Sinon, that base slave, made King Priam think Epeus' pine tree horse was a sacrifice to appease the wrath of Minerva. In addition, Priam believed Sinon's words because the Trojan Laocoon threw and broke a spear on the hollow breast of the Trojan Horse, after which two winged serpents stung him to death."

Minerva was said to be angry because Ulysses and Diomedes had broken into Troy and had stolen a statue of her.

Aeneas continued:

"Aghast at Laocoon's death, we were commanded immediately to draw the Trojan Horse with reverence into Troy. In this unhappy work I myself was employed. These hands did help to haul it to the gates, through which it could not enter because it was so huge.

"Oh, if it had never entered Troy, Troy would still stand today! But King Priam, impatient of delay, ordered that a wide breach be made in that fortified wall, which a thousand battering rams could never pierce, and so came in this fatal, deadly instrument, at whose accursed feet, overjoyed we banqueted until, overcome with wine, some grew ill and others soundly slept.

"Seeing this, Sinon caused the Greek spies to hasten to Tenedos and tell the military camp. Then he unlocked the Trojan Horse, and suddenly from out its entrails Neoptolemus, the son of Achilles, setting his spear upon the ground, leaped forth, and after him came a thousand more Greek soldiers, in whose stern faces shined the quenchless fire that soon burnt the pride of Asia.

"By this time, the Greek army had come to the Trojan walls, and through the breach we had made they marched into the streets, where, meeting with the Greek warriors who had exited from the Trojan Horse, they cried, 'Kill! Kill!'

"Frightened by this confused noise, I rose, and looking from a turret, I saw young infants swimming in their parents' blood, headless carcasses piled up in heaps, half-dead virgins dragged by their golden hair and with main force flung on a ring of pikes, and old men with swords thrust through their aged sides, kneeling for mercy in front of Greek lads who with steel poleaxes dashed out their brains.

"Then I buckled on my armor and drew my sword, thinking to go down and fight, but suddenly came Hector's ghost, with an ashy visage and bluish sulfurous eyes, his arms torn from his shoulders, and his breast furrowed with wounds, and — something that made me weep — thongs at his heels, by which Achilles' horse drew him in triumph through the Greek camp."

After Achilles had killed Hector in single combat, he cut holes in his feet through which he tied thongs so that he could drag Hector's corpse behind his horse.

Aeneas continued:

"Yes, Hector's ghost burst from the earth, crying 'Aeneas, flee! Troy is on fire! The Greeks have conquered the town!'"

Dido said, "Oh, Hector, who does not weep when they hear your name!"

Aeneas continued:

"Despite Hector's words, I flung myself forth, and desperate concerning my life, I ran into the thickest throngs of the enemy and with this sword sent many of their savage souls to hell.

"At last came Pyrrhus, son of Achilles, deadly and full of anger, his armor dropping blood, and on his spear the mangled head of Priam's youngest son, and after him came his band of Myrmidons, with balls of wild-fire — incendiaries — in their murdering paws, which made the funeral flame that burnt fair Troy. All of them hemmed me about, crying, 'This is he.'"

"Ah, how could poor Aeneas escape their hands?" Dido asked.

Aeneas continued:

"My mother, Venus, very protective of my health, conveyed me away from their malignant nets and bonds. So I escaped the furious wrath of Pyrrhus, who then ran to King Priam's palace, and at Jove's altar finding Priam, about whose withered neck hung Hecuba, enfolding his hand in hers, and jointly both beating their breasts and falling on the ground.

"Pyrrhus, with his sword's point raised up at once, and with the eyes of Megaera, one of the Furies, stared in their faces, threatening a thousand deaths at every glance.

"To Pyrrhus the aged King Priam, trembling, said, 'Achilles' son, remember what I was, father of fifty sons, but they are slain; lord of my fortune, but my fortune's turned; King of this city, but my Troy is on fire; and now I am not father, lord, or King. Yet who is so wretched but they still desire to live? Oh, let me live, great Neoptolemus!'"

Neoptolemus is another name for Achilles' son, Pyrrhus.

Aeneas continued:

"Not moved at all, but smiling at Priam's tears, this butcher, Pyrrhus, while Priam's hands were yet held up, treading upon his breast, used his sword to cut off his hands."

"Oh, stop, Aeneas!" Dido said. "I can bear to hear no more."

Aeneas continued:

"At this the frantic Queen Hecuba leaped on Pyrrhus' face, and in his eyelids hanging by the fingernails, for a little while prolonged her husband's life. At last the soldiers pulled her by the heels and swung her howling in the empty air, which sent an echo to the wounded King Priam. Hearing the cries of his wife, he lifted up his bed-ridden limbs, and would have grappled with Achilles' son, forgetting both his lack of strength and his loss of hands.

"Pyrrhus, feeling contempt for the aged King, whisked his sword about in the air, and the wind the sword created caused the King to fall down. Then from the navel to the throat at once Pyrrhus ripped old Priam, at whose last gasps Jove's marble statue began to bend the brow and scowl to show his loathing of Pyrrhus for this wicked act.

"Yet Pyrrhus, undaunted, took his father's battle flag and dipped it in the old King's chill, cold blood, and then in triumph he ran into the streets, through which he could not pass because they were choked with slaughtered men.

"So, leaning on his sword, Pyrrhus stood stone still, viewing the fire wherewith rich Ilion — Troy — burned.

"By this time, I had gotten my father on my back, gotten this young boy who is now sitting on your lap in my arms, and, was leading fair Creusa, my beloved wife, by the hand."

This sounds as if Aeneas had a third arm, but this is how he told the story.

Aeneas looked at Achates and said, "We met up with you, Achates, and while you with your sword made a way for us, and while we were surrounded by the Greeks, oh, there I lost my wife. If we had not fought manfully, I would not have lived to tell this tale.

"Yet manhood would not serve to achieve victory. We were forced to flee, and as we went to our ships, you know that we saw sprawling in the streets Cassandra, whom Little Ajax raped in Diana's temple. Her cheeks were swollen with sighs, her hair was all torn, and I took her up to carry her to our ships."

This sounds as if Aeneas were now carrying his father, his son, and Cassandra, but that is how he told the story.

Aeneas continued:

"But suddenly the Greeks followed us, and I, alas, was forced to let her lie. Then we got to our ships, and once we were aboard, from the shore Polyxena, one of Priam's daughters, cried out, 'Aeneas, wait! The Greeks pursue me. Stay and take me in your ship!'

"Moved by her voice, I leaped into the sea, thinking to bear her on my back aboard, for all our ships were launched into the sea, and as I swam, she, standing on the shore, was by the cruel Myrmidons surprised and captured and afterward Pyrrhus made a human sacrifice of her."

Dido said, "I die with melting pity. Aeneas, stop."

Dido's sister, Anna, asked, "Oh, what became of aged Hecuba?"

Iarbas asked, "How did Aeneas get to the fleet again?"

Dido asked, "How did Helen, who caused this war, escape?"

Aeneas said, "Achates, speak. Sorrow has quite tired me."

Achates said, "What happened to Queen Hecuba, we cannot tell. We hear they led her captive into Greece. As for Aeneas, he swam quickly back to the ship. Helena betrayed Deiphobus, who had become her lover after Alexander, aka Paris, died, and so she was reconciled to Menelaus."

"Oh, I wish that enticing strumpet had never been born!" Dido said about Helen. "Trojan, your pity-arousing tale has made me sad. Come, let us think about some pleasing entertainment to rid me of these melancholy thoughts."

They began to exit. As they were exiting, Venus showed up with Cupid, her son.

Venus took Ascanius, Aeneas' son, by the sleeve, making him stay behind as the others left.

Pretending to be one of Dido's serving women, she said to him, "Fair child, stay with me, Dido's waiting maid. I'll give you sugar almonds, sweet candied fruits, a silver belt, and a golden wallet."

Pointing at Cupid, she added, "And this young Prince shall be your playfellow."

"Are you Queen Dido's son?" Ascanius asked.

"Yes," Cupid lied, adding, "and my mother gave me this fine bow." He nearly always carried a bow and a quiver of golden arrows.

"Shall I have such a quiver and a bow?" Ascanius asked.

"Dido will give to sweet Ascanius such a bow, such a quiver, and such golden shafts," Venus said. "For Dido's sake I now take you in my arms and stick these feathers, which are sparkling because bits of metal are embedded in them, in your hat. Eat candied fruits in my arms, and I will sing to you."

She sang Ascanius a lullaby, and he fell asleep.

Venus said, "Now is he fast asleep, and in this grove among green bushes I'll lay Ascanius and strew sweet-smelling violets, blushing roses, and purple hyacinth over him. These milk-white doves shall be his sentinels; if anyone seeks to hurt him, these doves will quickly fly to Venus' fist."

In addition to their other superpowers, the gods and goddesses are shape-shifters. Cupid also had the superpower of making people fall in love by shooting — or merely scratching — them with one of his arrows.

Venus said, "Now, Cupid, turn yourself into Ascanius' shape and go to Dido, who instead of him will set you on her lap and play with you. Then touch her white breast with this arrowhead, so that she may dote upon Aeneas' love, and by that means repair his broken ships, feed his soldiers, and give him wealthy gifts. He at last will depart to go to Italy, or else make his kingly throne in Carthage."

"I will, fair mother," Cupid said, "and I will so play my part that every touch shall wound Queen Dido's heart."

Cupid exited.

Venus set Ascanius down amid some bushes and said, "Sleep, my sweet grandson, in these cooling shades, free from the murmur of these running streams, the cry of beasts, the rattling of the winds, and the whisking of these leaves. All shall be still and nothing shall interrupt your quiet sleep until I return and take you away from here again."

CHAPTER 3

— 3.1 —

Cupid alone, disguised as Ascanius, said to himself, "Now, Cupid, cause the Carthaginian Queen to be enamored of your half-brother's looks."

Venus was the mother of both Aeneas and Cupid by different fathers, and so they were half-brothers.

Cupid continued, "Carry this golden arrow in your sleeve, lest she realize you are Venus' son, and when she strokes you softly on the head, then I shall touch her breast with this arrow and conquer her."

He would conquer her by making her fall in love with Aeneas.

Iarbas, Anna, and Dido entered the room.

Iarbas asked, "How long, fair Dido, shall I pine for you? It is not enough that you grant me love, for I need to enjoy what I desire. That love is childish that consists only of words."

Dido replied, "Iarbas, know that you of all my wooers (and yet I have had many mightier Kings wooing me) have had the greatest favors I could give you. I fear that I, Dido, have been thought to be promiscuous because I have been too familiar with Iarbas, although the gods know no wanton thought has ever had residence in Dido's breast."

"But Dido is the favor I request," Iarbas said.

Dido replied, "Don't fear, Iarbas. Dido may be yours."

"Look, sister," Anna said. "Look at how Aeneas' little son plays with your garments and embraces you."

Tugging at Dido's skirt, the disguised Cupid said, "No, Dido will not take me in her arms; I shall not be her son, for she does not love me."

"Don't cry, sweet boy," Dido said. "You shall be Dido's son. Sit in my lap, and let me hear you sing."

The disguised Cupid sang a childish song.

"No more, my child," Dido said. "Now talk for a little while, and tell me where you learned this pretty song."

"My cousin Helen taught it to me in Troy," the disguised Cupid said.

"How lovely Ascanius is when he smiles," Dido said.

The disguised Cupid asked, "Will Dido let me hang about her neck?"

"Yes, waggish boy, and she gives you permission to kiss her, too."

"What will you give me now?" the disguised Cupid asked. "I'll have this fan."

The disguised Cupid took the fan, and as he did so, he lightly touched Dido with his golden arrow. Immediately, she fell in love with Aeneas. Her thoughts toward Iarbas wavered between completely rejecting him and treating him well.

"Take it, Ascanius, for your father's sake," Dido said.

"Come, Dido, leave Ascanius," Iarbas said. "Let us walk together."

"You, go away," Dido said. "Ascanius shall stay."

"Unkind, cruel Queen, is this how you show your love for me?" Iarbas said.

He started to leave.

"Oh, stay, Iarbas, and I'll go with you," Dido said.

Iarbas stayed.

"And if my mother goes, I'll follow her," the disguised Cupid said. By "mother," he meant Dido. Ascanius had earlier told her that she would be his mother.

Dido asked Iarbas, "Why do you stay here? You are no love of mine."

"Iarbas, die, seeing that Dido abandons you," Iarbas said.

"No, Iarbas, live," Dido said. "What have you done that you deserve that I should say you are no love of mine? Nothing."

She immediately changed her mind: "Yes, you have done something that made you deserve it. Go away, I say! Depart from Carthage. Don't come within my sight."

"Am I not King of rich Gaetulia?" Iarbas asked.

Dido replied, "Iarbas, pardon me and stay a while."

"Mother, look here," the disguised Cupid said.

Dido again changed her mind: "Why are you telling me about rich Gaetulia? Am I not Queen of Libya? So then depart."

"I am leaving to satisfy this weird mood of yours, my love," Iarbas said. "Yet I will not go from Carthage for a thousand worlds."

Iarbas started to leave.

Dido changed her mind and called his name: "Iarbas!"

Iarbas turned around and asked, "Did Dido call me back?"

Dido again changed her mind and said, "No, but I order you never again to look at me."

"Then pull out both of my eyes, or let me die," Iarbas said.

He exited.

Anna asked Dido, her sister, "For what reason did Dido tell Iarbas to leave?"

"Because his loathsome sight offends my eye," Dido said, "and because in my thoughts is enshrined another love. Oh, Anna, if you knew how sweet love is, very soon you would abjure this single life."

Anna replied, "Poor soul, I know too well the sour of love. Oh, I wish that Iarbas could fancy me!"

"Isn't Aeneas fair and beautiful?" Dido asked.

"Yes, and Iarbas is foul and favorless," Anna said.

"Favorless" means "unattractive."

Anna may have been merely indulging the mood of her sister, or she may have been actively trying to make Dido no longer love Iarbas, whom Anna herself loved.

"Isn't Aeneas eloquent in all his speech?" Dido asked.

"Yes, and Iarbas is rude and rustic in his speech," Anna replied.

"Don't say the name 'Iarbas.' But sweet Anna, tell me, isn't Aeneas worthy of Dido's love?"

"Oh, sister," Anna said, "even if you were Empress of the world, Aeneas would well deserve to be your love. So lovely is he that wherever he goes, the people swarm to gaze at his face."

"But tell them that none but I shall gaze on him, lest their gross eyebeams taint my lover's cheeks," Dido said.

This society's theory of vision was that eyes shot out beams that allowed the eyes to see objects. Being stared at by a lower-class person could therefore taint an upper-class person.

Dido continued, "Anna, good sister Anna, go to him and bring him here, lest I melt clean away with these sweet thoughts."

"Then, sister, you'll abjure Iarbas' love?" Anna asked.

"Must I hear that loathsome name yet again?" Dido asked.

"Run for Aeneas, or I'll fly to him."

The disguised Cupid said, "You shall not hurt my father when he comes."

"No, I won't," Dido replied. "For your sake I'll love your father well."

She then said to herself, "Oh, dull-brained Dido, who until now did never think Aeneas to be beautiful! But now, for quittance of this oversight, I'll make myself bracelets of his golden hair. His glistening eyes shall be my looking glass. His lips shall be an altar where I'll offer up as many kisses as the sea has grains of sands. Instead of music I will hear him speak. His looks shall be my only library, and you, Aeneas, shall be Dido's treasury, in whose fair bosom I will lock more wealth than twenty thousand Indias can afford.

"Oh, here he comes! Love, love, give Dido the ability to be more modest than her thoughts admit, lest I be made a wonder to the world."

Dido was worried about being the object of gossip.

Aeneas, accompanied by his fellow Trojans Achates, Cloanthus, Ilioneus, and Sergestus entered.

Pretending that she had not seen Aeneas, Dido asked, "Achates, how does Carthage please your lord?"

Achates motioned toward Aeneas and replied, "That is something Aeneas can tell your majesty."

"Aeneas, are you there?" Dido asked.

"I understand that your highness sent for me," Aeneas replied.

"No," Dido lied, "but now that you are here, tell me truly what Dido might do to highly please you."

"So much have I received from Dido's hands that I can ask for no more without blushing," Aeneas replied, "yet still, Queen of Africa, my ships are unrigged, my sails all torn apart by the wind, my oars broken, and my tackling lost. Yes, all the ships of my navy are split because of rocks and sandbars. Our maimed fleet has neither rudders nor anchors. Our masts the furious winds struck overboard. If Dido will supply us with these things we so piteously lack, we will account her the author of our lives."

God is often considered the author of all life. Aeneas was saying that if Dido would outfit his ships, he and the other Trojans would regard her as a goddess.

Dido replied, "Aeneas, I'll repair your Trojan ships, on the condition that you will stay with me and let Achates sail to Italy.

"I'll give you tackling made of twisted gold thread wound on the barks of odoriferous, sweet-smelling trees.

"I'll give you oars of massy ivory, full of holes through which the water shall delight to play."

Dido seems to have not known a thing about rowing. Or she may have meant that the oars she would give to Aeneas himself in particular would have holes so that they would be ineffective in taking him away from her.

She continued, "Your anchors shall be hewed from crystal rocks so that, if you loose or lose them, they shall shine above the waves."

When anchors are loosed, they are brought up from the ocean's floor to be stored on ship. Once above the waves, Aeneas' anchor would shine brightly. In addition, as Achates sailed away and Aeneas "lost" his ships, Aeneas could long see the shining anchors.

Dido continued:

"The masts whereon your swelling sails shall hang will be hollow obelisks of silver plate.

"The sails will be made of fine cloth folded over for thickness, and embroidered on the sails shall be scenes of the wars of Troy, but not of Troy's overthrow."

She may have been thinking that thicker sails would blow the ships faster away from Carthage and Dido — and Aeneas.

Dido continued, "As for ballast, empty Dido's treasury."

She then said to Achates:

"Take what you will, but leave Aeneas here. Achates, you shall be so manly clad that sea-born nymphs shall swarm about your ships and wanton mermaids shall court you with sweet songs, flinging into your ship gifts of more sovereign worth than Thetis hangs about Apollo's neck, provided that Aeneas may stay with me."

Thetis is a sea-goddess who is the mother of the Greek Achilles, the strongest and best warrior of the Trojan War.

Apollo is the sun-god.

Aeneas asked, "Why would Dido have Aeneas stay here in Carthage?"

"To war against my bordering enemies," Dido said. "Aeneas, don't think that Dido is in love, for if any man could conquer me, I would have been wedded before Aeneas came to Carthage."

She pointed to a wall and said, "Look where the pictures of my suitors hang. Aren't these suitors as fair as fair may be?"

"I saw this man at Troy, before Troy was sacked," Achates said.

"I saw this man in Greece when Paris stole fair Helen," Aeneas said.

"This man and I were at Olympus' games," Illioneus said.

"I know this face," Sergestus said. "He is a Persian born. I traveled with him to Aetolia."

"And I, unless I am deceived, disputed with this gentleman once in Athens about a philosophical matter," Cloanthus said.

Dido pointed to another group of pictures and said, "But speak, Aeneas. Do you know any of these men?"

"No, madam, but it seems that these men are Kings," Aeneas replied.

Dido said, "All these and others whom I never saw have been most urgent suitors for my love. Some suitors came in person, and others sent their legates, yet none obtained me. I am free from all."

She thought, *And yet, God knows, I am entangled to one: you, Aeneas.*

As she spoke, she pointed to various pictures:

"This man was an orator and thought by words to win me, but yet he was deceived.

"And this man is a Spartan courtier, vain and wild, but his fantastic moods did not please me.

"This man was Alcion, a musician, but despite how sweetly he played, I let him go.

"This man was the wealthy King of Thessaly, but I had gold enough and cast him off.

"This man was Meleager's son, a warlike Prince, but weapons don't agree with my tender years.

"The rest are such as all the world well knows, yet now I swear, by heaven and by him I love, I was as far from loving as they were from hating."

Aeneas said, "Oh, happy shall he be whom Dido loves."

"Then never say that you are miserable, because it may be you shall be my love," Dido said. "Yet don't boast about it, for I do not love you. And yet I do not hate you."

She thought, *Oh, if I speak, I shall betray myself. Aeneas, you speak.*

Dido continued, "We two will go hunting in the woods, but not so much for you — you are only one person — as for Achates and his followers."

Juno looked at Ascanius, who was asleep in the midst of thick bushes, and she said, "Here lies my hate, Aeneas' cursed brat, the boy wherein treacherous destiny delights, the heir of Fame, the favorite of Fate, that ugly imp that shall outlast my wrath and wrong my deity with high disgrace."

Ascanius' destiny was to go to Italy with his father, and along with his father, become an important ancestor of the Roman people.

Juno continued, "But I will take another order now and raze and erase the eternal register of time."

She wanted to change what was fated to occur.

She continued, "Troy shall no more call Ascanius her second hope, nor shall Venus triumph in his tender youth, for here, in spite of heaven, I'll murder him and feed infection with his left-out life."

She wanted to murder him and to allow his stinking corpse — his body with his life left out — to infect the air.

Juno continued, "Say, Paris, now shall Venus have the ball? Say, Vengeance, shall her Ascanius die now?"

One reason why Juno hated the Trojans was the Judgment of Paris. Three goddesses — Juno, Minerva, and Venus — held a beauty contest with Paris, Prince of Troy, as the judge. The prize for the winner was a golden ball, often referred to as a golden apple. Each goddess attempted to bribe Paris to choose her, and Paris accepted Venus' bribe: Helen, the most beautiful woman in the world. Helen was already married to Menelaus, King of Sparta, and Paris went to Sparta and ran away with Helen. Ancient authorities disagree about whether Helen went with Paris willingly.

Juno, however, had second thoughts about murdering a sleeping, innocent young boy:

"Oh, no! God knows, I cannot take advantage of this opportunity, nor requite with a double payment the 'good turns' — the insults —

done to me. Bah, I am foolish, without a mind able to hurt this child, and I have no gall at all to use to aggrieve my foe, but lustful Jove and his adulterous child — Venus, who had an affair with Mars, the god of war — shall find it written on Confusion's forehead that only Juno rules in the town of Rhamnus."

Rhamnus, a town in Attica, was the site of a major shrine to Nemesis, goddess of vengeance and punishment. Juno meant that even though she could not kill Ascanius, she would still find a way to get major vengeance for what she considered major wrongs done to her.

Venus arrived, saying to herself, "What does this mean? My doves returned to me, and they warn me of such danger close at hand — danger that would harm my sweet Ascanius' lovely life."

Seeing Juno, Venus said, "Juno, my mortal foe, what are you doing here? Leave, old witch, and don't trouble my mind."

"For shame, Venus, that such words of wrath should without a reason ever defile so fair a mouth as yours," Juno said. "Aren't we both sprung of a celestial race, aren't we both goddesses, and don't we both banquet as two sisters with the gods? Why then should displeasure disjoin us two whom kinship and acquaintance do unite?"

"Out, hateful hag!" Venus said. "You would have slain my grandson, except that my sacred doves discovered your intention and came to me. But I will tear your eyes from out of your head and feast the birds with the bloodshot eyeballs, if you but lay your fingers on my boy Ascanius."

"Is this then all the thanks that I shall have for saving him from snakes' and serpents' fangs that would have killed him, sleeping as he lay?" Juno said. "So what if I was offended with your son, and wrought him much woe on sea and land, when, because of my hatred for Trojan Ganymede, who was advanced by my Hebe's shame — Jupiter made Ganymede his cupbearer, taking that honor from my daughter Hebe — and because of my hatred for Paris' judgment of the heavenly ball, I mustered all the winds to wreck Aeneas' fleet and urged each element — earth, air, fire, and water — to do him harm.

"Yet now I repent of causing his sorrow and I wish that I had never wronged him so. It is useless, I see now, to war with fate, which has so many irresistible friends, and therefore I changed my counsel with the time and have planted love where malice formerly had sprung."

"Sister of Jove, if it is true that your love is such now as you protest it is, we two as friends will divide one fortune," Venus said.

Juno was both Jupiter's sister and his wife.

Venus continued, "Cupid shall lay his arrows in your lap and exchange his golden shafts for a scepter — that will show that he is a follower of yours. Fancy love and modesty — the fanciful amour of young lovers and the modesty of wives — shall live as mates, and fair peacocks, which are sacred to you, shall perch by doves, which are sacred to me. Love my Aeneas, and desire, which I control since I am the goddess of sexual passion, is yours. The day, the night, my swans, my sweets, are yours."

"More than melodious are these words to me, these words that overfill my soul with their content," Juno replied. "Venus, sweet Venus, how may I deserve such amorous favors from your beauteous hand?"

As the goddess of sexual passion, Venus could either help or hurt Juno. She could hurt Juno, a jealous wife, by making Jupiter fall in love with goddesses and mortal women. Or she could help Juno by making Jupiter fall and stay in love only with Juno.

Juno continued, "But so that you may more easily perceive how highly I prize this amity and friendship, listen to a motion of eternal league, which I will make as a reward for your love and friendship.

"Your son Aeneas, you know, now remains with Dido and feeds his eyes with favors of her court and courtship. She likewise spends her time in admiring him and can neither talk nor think of anything but him.

"Why shouldn't they then join in marriage and bring forth mighty Kings to rule Carthage, these two whom a chance occurrence of the sea has made such friends?"

It wasn't really a chance occurrence that made Aeneas come to the shore of Carthage; Juno had arranged for the storm that damaged the ships of Aeneas' fleet.

Juno continued, "And, Venus, let there be a match confirmed between these two whose loves are so alike, and we two goddesses, working together as one, shall chain felicity to their throne."

Venus replied, "I could well like this means of reconcilement, but I much fear that my son will never consent because metaphorically his armed soul, already on the sea, darts forth her light to Lavinia's shore."

She meant that Aeneas was still thinking about Italy. His soul is armed in case he needs to fight to establish himself there. Lavinia is the Italian woman whom he is fated to marry.

Juno said, "Fair Queen of love, I will divorce these doubts and find the way to weary such foolish thoughts. You need not worry: I will make Aeneas stop thinking about Italy.

"Today Aeneas and Dido will go forth to hunt and will ride into these woods next to these walls. When they are in the midst of all their entertaining sports, I'll make the clouds discharge their water and drench Silvanus' dwellings with their showers."

Silvanus is the god of woodlands and fields.

Juno continued, "Then in one cave Queen Dido and Aeneas shall meet and mutually disclose their thoughts to each other, and quickly their hearts will be sealed with vows of love. Marriage will follow, I am sure, just as we propose."

Venus said, "Sister, I see you savor of my wiles."

Venus and Cupid were usually the ones whose wiles led to people falling in love. Juno, however, was doing a fine job of that right now.

Venus continued, "Be it as you will have it for this once. In the meantime Ascanius shall be my responsibility. I will bear him to the

Idalian groves in Cyprus in my arms, and bed him in Adonis' purple down."

Adonis' "purple down" was the purple flowers known as anemones. While he was hunting, a boar gored and killed him. From his blood grew purple anemones.

Dido, Aeneas, Anna, Iarbas, Achates, the disguised Cupid, and some others met, ready to go hunting or to assist in the hunting.

"Aeneas, know that I honor you by thus in person going with you to hunt. My princely robes, as you can see, are laid aside. The glittering pomp of those clothes Diana's outfit now supplies."

Diana was the goddess of the hunt, and her clothing was the clothing of hunters.

Dido continued, "All of us are fellow hunters now, and we are all disposed alike to sport. The woods are wide, and we have plenty of game."

She said, "Aeneas, handsome Trojan, hold my golden bow a while until I tie my quiver to my side.

"Lords, go on ahead of us. We two — Aeneas and I — must talk alone."

Iarbus said to himself, "Cruel woman, can she wrong Iarbas so? I'll die before I allow a foreigner to treat me so cruelly. 'We two will talk alone' — what words are these?"

"What makes Iarbas stay here away from all the rest?" Dido said. "We can do without your company."

"Perhaps love and duty led him on," Aeneas said, "to remain within your sight despite your opposition."

"Why, man of Troy, do I offend your eyes?" Iarbus asked. "Or are you grieved that your betters come so near to Dido?"

"What is this, Gaetulian!" an angry Dido said. "Have you grown so bold that you challenge us with your comparisons? Do you think that you are better than Aeneas? Peasant, go seek companions like yourself, and don't meddle with anyone whom I love and respect.

"Aeneas, don't be angered by what he says, for now and again he will be out of joint."

Iarbus said to himself, "Women may wrong others by the privilege of love; a man who loves a woman will take much abuse from her. But if Aeneas, that 'man of men' — or anyone except Dido — had taunted me with these opprobrious terms, I would have either drunk Aeneas' dying blood immediately, or else I would have offered a challenge to Aeneas to fight to the death in single combat."

Dido said, "Huntsmen, why don't you set up your nets quickly and rouse the light-footed deer from out of their lair?"

Anna said to Dido, "Sister, look. See Ascanius in his pomp, bearing his hunting spear bravely in his hand."

"Hey, little son, are you so eager now?" Dido asked.

The disguised Cupid replied, "Yes, mother, I shall one day be a man, and better able unto other arms."

His words were ambiguous. The innocent meaning was that he would be a man and would be able to wield arms — hunting weapons — much better than he could now. The bawdy meaning was that he would be a man and would be able to render good service within other arms — the arms of a woman.

Cupid's words, however, applied only to Ascanius, who would grow up to be a warrior and have children. Cupid would never grow up. Gods and goddesses were born, and then grew to a certain age, which varied for each of them, and then stopped aging. Jupiter would always be a mature man. Mercury would always be a young man. Cupid would always be a young boy.

He continued, "Meanwhile these wanton weapons serve my war, and I will break my spear between a lion's jaws."

Of course, they were hunting deer, not lions, but these were brave words.

"What!" Dido said, laughing. "Do you dare to look a lion in the face?"

"Yes, and I will outface him, too, no matter what he does," the disguised Cupid said.

"How like his father he speaks in all he says," Anna said.

Aeneas said, "And if I could live to see him sack rich Thebes and load his spear with the heads of Greek Princes, then I would wish that I were with my late father, Anchises, in his tomb, and dead. That way I could bring news of Ascanius' actions to honor the father who has brought me up."

Iarbus said to himself, "And if I could live to see you, Aeneas, shipped away and hoisted aloft on the sea-god Neptune's hideous hills — the sea's tall waves — then I would wish that I were in fair Dido's arms and dead."

To "die" in a woman's arms meant to have an orgasm while in her arms.

Iarbus continued, "That way I would scorn that which has pursued me so."

What was pursuing Iarbus was jealousy of Aeneas.

Aeneas said, "Brave friend, Achates, do you know this wood?"

"I remember that here you shot the deer that saved your famished soldiers' lives from death, when first you set your foot upon the shore," Achates replied. "And here we met fair Venus, disguised as a human maiden, bearing her bow and quiver at her back."

Remembering past troubles that he and his fellow Trojans had overcome, Aeneas said, "Oh, how these irksome labors now delight and overjoy my thoughts because of our escape from them. Who would not undergo all kinds of toil to be well stored with such a winter's tale?"

Stories of past troubles well overcome are good to tell on a winter's evening.

Dido said, "Aeneas, leave these reveries and let's all go. Some go to the mountains, and some go to the wetlands. You people go to the valleys."

Then to Iarbus, she said, insultingly, "You go to the house."

Everyone except Iarbas exited.

He said to himself, "Yes, this it is that wounds me to the death: To see a Trojan Phrygian, fetched from far over the sea, preferred before a man of majesty — me!

"Oh, love! Oh, hate! Oh, cruel women's hearts, that imitate the moon in every change and like the planets always love to range."

According to Iarbus, women's hearts are ever changeable like the moon, and they wander from man to man like the planets wander in the night sky.

He continued, "What shall I do, I who am thus wronged with Dido's disdain? Should I get revenge on Aeneas or on her? On her? Foolish man, getting revenge on her would be the equivalent of going to war against the gods of heaven. My shooting one arrow would provoke the gods into throwing ten thousand spears at me.

"Iarbus, this Trojan's death will be your malice's goal. His blood will make you happy again and will make love drunken with your sweet desire.

"But Dido, who now thinks of him so dearly, will 'die' with hearing the news of his death.

"But time will discontinue her love for Aeneas and mold her mind unto new fancy's shapes. She will lose her love for Aeneas and seek a new man to love — women's hearts are changeable! Oh, God of heaven, turn the hand of Fate to that happy day of my delight!

"And then — what then? Iarbas shall only love. So does he now, though not with equal gain. That rests in your rival, who causes your pain — Aeneas, who will never cease to soar until he is slain."

Juno caused a storm, and first Dido and then Aeneas sought shelter in the same cave.

"Aeneas!" Dido said.

"Dido!" Aeneas said.

"Tell me, dear love, how did you find this cave?" Dido asked.

"By chance, sweet Queen, just like Mars and Venus met."

He was referring to a story in which Mars and Venus committed adultery. Venus was married to Vulcan, a master blacksmith who found out about the adultery and created a fine net in which he trapped them in the act of love-making and then invited the other gods to come and laugh at them.

Vulcan had created a trap for Venus and Mars, and Juno had set a trap for Dido and Aeneas.

Dido said, "Why, that was in a net, whereas we are loose."

"Loose" can mean "promiscuous."

She continued, "And yet I am not free. Oh, I wish I were!"

"Why, what is it that Dido may desire and not obtain, as long as it is in human power to obtain?" Aeneas asked.

"The thing that I will die before I ask for, and yet desire to have before I die," Dido said.

Another meaning of the verb "die" is "have an orgasm."

"Is it anything Aeneas may get for you?" he asked.

"Aeneas?" Dido said. "No, although his eyes do pierce."

She wanted another part of his body to pierce her.

"Has Iarbas angered her in anything, and will she be avenged on his life?" Aeneas asked, referring to Dido in the third person.

"He has not angered me, except in angering you," Dido replied.

"Who, then, of all men so cruel may he be that he should make you notice his defects?" Aeneas asked.

"The man whom I see wherever I am, whose amorous face, like the face of Paean — Apollo, god of the sun — sparkles fire, when he shoots his beams on Flora's bed."

Flora is the goddess of gardens and flowers, and so her bed is the earth.

Dido continued, "Prometheus has put on Cupid's shape, and I must perish in his burning arms."

Prometheus brought the gift of fire to human beings, and Cupid causes human beings to fall in love. Dido was saying that Aeneas was like a combination of these gods and that he was so magnificent that she would die in his arms.

Again, "the verb "die" means "have an orgasm."

"Aeneas, oh, Aeneas, quench these flames!" Dido said.

"What ails my Queen?" Aeneas said. "Has she fallen sick recently?"

"Not sick, my love," Dido said.

She thought, *But I am lovesick. I must conceal the torment that it will not profit me to reveal. ... And yet I'll speak. ... And yet I'll hold my peace. ... Let Shame do her worst. I will disclose my grief.*

She said out loud, "Aeneas, you are the man I mean. What did I say? Something it was that now I have forgotten."

"What does fair Dido mean by this unclear speech?" Aeneas asked.

"Oh, nothing," Dido said. "But Aeneas does not love me."

"Aeneas' thoughts dare not ascend so high as Dido's heart, which monarchs might not scale," Aeneas said.

Aeneas was not a King. As a Queen, Dido would be expected to marry a King.

Dido said, "It was because I saw no King like you, whose golden crown might balance and equal my happiness — you are the man who can make me happy. But now that I have found the man whom I should love, I follow a man who loves Fame more than he loves me, a man who would rather seem fair to the eyes of Sirens than to the Carthage Queen who dies for him."

The Sirens sang beautifully to lure sailors to crash their ships on rocks.

Dido continued, "I love a man who would rather sail to Italy than stay at Carthage with me."

"If your majesty can look so low as my despised worths that shun all praise," Aeneas said, "with this my hand I give to you my heart and I vow by all the gods of hospitality, by heaven and earth, by my fair half-brother's bow, by Paphos, Capys, and the purple sea from whence my radiant mother descended, and by this sword that saved me from the Greeks, never to leave these newly built walls of Carthage, while Dido lives and rules in Juno's favorite town. I vow never to like or love any but her."

Aeneas was swearing a mighty oath. He was swearing by the gods of hospitality, especially Jupiter but also Mercury. He was also swearing by heaven and earth and by the bow of his half-brother, Cupid. He was also swearing by Paphos, where was located a temple to his mother, Venus. He was also swearing by his grandparents. Capys was his father's father, and his mother was born from the foam of the purple sea by Cythera and then traveled to Cyprus.

"What more than Delian music do I hear, music that calls my soul from forth his living seat — my heart — to dance to the measures of delight!" Dido said.

Delos is the birthplace of Apollo, god of music.

She continued, "Kind clouds that sent forth such a courteous storm as made disdain to flee to love's lap! Valiant love, in my arms make your Italy, whose crown and kingdom rest at your command. You shall command my body. Sichaeus, not Aeneas, shall you be called — you shall be called by the name of my late husband. You shall be called the King of Carthage, not the son of Anchises."

To love Dido and stay with her in Carthage would cost Aeneas much of his identity — and his destiny.

Dido continued, "Wait. Take these jewels from the hand of your lover, me. Take these golden bracelets, and this wedding ring with which my husband wooed me, while I was still a maiden, and be King of Libya by my gift."

They went deeper into the cave.

CHAPTER 4
— 4.1 —

Achates, Cupid (still disguised as Ascanius), Iarbas, and Anna stood together after the storm.

"Have men ever seen such a sudden storm, or a day that was so clear become so suddenly overcast?" Achates asked.

"I think some powerful enchantress dwells here," Iarbus said, "who can call storms forth whenever she pleases and dive into black tempest's treasury whenever she means to mask the world with clouds."

"In all my life I never knew the like," Anna said. "It hailed; it snowed; it lightninged all at once."

"I think it was the devil's night to revel," Achates said. "There was such hurly-burly in the heavens. Doubtless Apollo's axle-tree cracked, or aged Atlas' shoulder got out of joint, the commotion was so excessively violent."

If the axle of Apollo's sun-chariot were to crack, he would have to repair it and the sun would be out of commission for a while, leading to the darkness of storms on the Earth.

Atlas was the Titan who held up the sky. If his shoulder were to get out of joint, he would have to adjust the sky on his shoulders, causing atmospheric disturbances.

"In all this turmoil, where have you left Queen Dido?" Iarbus asked.

"And where's my warlike father, can you tell me?" the disguised Cupid asked.

Seeing them, Anna said, "Look where both of them are coming out of the cave."

"Coming out of the cave!" Iarbus said.

He knew they had been alone together, and knowing that Dido loved Aeneas, he could guess that they had had sex.

He said to himself, "Can heaven endure this sight? Iarbas, curse that unrevenging Jove, whose flinty darts slept in Typhon's den, while these adulterers surfeited with sin."

Iarbus was angry because Jupiter, whom he worshipped, had not punished the fornicating Aeneas and Dido with his "flinty darts," aka thunderbolts. Instead of hurling them at the couple, Jupiter had left the thunderbolts under Mount Etna, where Vulcan the blacksmith god manufactured them, using Mount Etna as his forge. Typhon was a monster that was imprisoned under Mount Etna.

Iarbus continued, "Nature, why didn't you make me some poisonous beast instead of making me human, so that with my sharp-edged fang I might have staked them both into the earth, while they were fornicating in this dark cave?"

Aeneas and Dido walked over to the others.

"The air is clear, and southern winds are calm and still," Aeneas said. "Come, Dido, let us hasten to the town, since gloomy Aeolus ceases to frown."

Aeolus, King of the winds, was no longer in a bad mood and so had stopped the storm.

"Achates and Ascanius, we are well met," Dido said. "It is good to see you."

"Fair Anna, how did you escape from the rain shower?" Aeneas asked.

"As others did, by running to the wood," Anna replied.

"But where were you, Iarbas, all this while?" Dido asked.

"Not with Aeneas in the ugly cave," he replied.

"I see Aeneas sticks in your mind, and you can't stop thinking about him," Dido said. "But I will soon put aside that stumbling block and quell those hopes that thus employ your thoughts."

Iarbas was preparing to sacrifice an animal to Jupiter. Some servants were with him.

"Come servants, come," Iarbus said. "Bring forth the sacrifice so that I may pacify that gloomy Jove, whose empty altars have enlarged our ills."

According to Iarbus, Jupiter was gloomy and inclined to punish Iarbus because Iarbus had not been making enough sacrifices to him.

The servants brought in the animal to be sacrificed and then exited.

Iarbus prayed, "Eternal Jove, great master of the clouds, you are the father of gladness and all frolicsome thoughts."

Jupiter dispenses both good things and bad things, and so he is the father of gladness although at times he can be gloomy.

Iarbus continued to pray: "You with your gloomy hand correct the heaven when airy creatures war amongst themselves."

"Airy creatures" include such things as the planets and other heavenly bodies. When necessary, Jupiter takes action to make things right when the airy creatures get out of hand. For example, when Phaethon drove the sun-chariot, he could not control the immortal horses that pulled it, and the sun got too close to the earth and nearly burned it (and likely could have burned other airy creatures). Jupiter restored order by killing Phaethon with a thunderbolt, and then Apollo took over driving the sun-chariot.

Iarbus continued to pray: "Hear, hear, oh, hear Iarbas' complaining prayers, whose hideous echoes make the welkin — the sky — howl and all the woods to resound with 'Eliza'!"

Queen Dido had other names, including Elissa and Eliza.

Iarbus continued to pray: "Dido is the woman whom you willed us to entertain and to treat well when, straying up and down our borders, she craved a hide of ground to build a town. With her we shared both laws and land and all the fruits that plenty also sends forth."

When Dido came to the shore of North Africa, she wanted land on which to build a city. She convinced Iarbus to allow her to purchase a hide's worth of land. He thought that she wanted to buy the amount of land that an animal hide would cover, but she cut the hide into very thin strips that she tied into a circle. The amount of land within the circle of animal hide strips was enough for her to build a city — Carthage — on.

That is according to one story. Possibly, a "hide" of land was a measure of land amounting to 100 or 120 acres.

Iarbus continued to pray: "Scorning our loves and royal marriage rites, Dido yields up her beauty to a foreigner's bed."

Many North African Kings had wooed Dido, who rejected them.

Iarbus continued to pray: "This foreigner, having wrought her shame, is straightway fled."

By agreeing to stay in Carthage with Dido, Aeneas had immediately fled from his destiny, which was to go to Italy, marry Lavinia, and become an important ancestor of the Roman people.

Iarbus continued to pray: "Now, if you are a pitying god of power, on whom pity and compassion forever attend, redress these wrongs and summon him to his ships. Take away from Africa this man who now afflicts me with his deceiving eyes."

Anna entered and said, "How are you now, Iarbas! At your prayers so hard?"

"Yes, Anna," Iarbus said. "Is there anything you want from me?"

"No," Anna said. "I have no such weighty business of importance, just what may be put off until another time. Yet, if you would share with me the cause of this devotion that detains you, I would be thankful to you for such courtesy."

"Anna, I am praying against this Trojan, Aeneas, who seeks to rob me of your sister's love and dive into her heart by false, deceiving looks."

"Alas, poor King, who labors so in vain for Dido, who so delights in your pain," Anna said. "Take my advice and seek some other love, a love whose yielding heart may yield you more relief."

"My eye is fixed on a woman whom I cannot make love me," Iarbus said. "Oh, leave me, leave me to my silent thoughts that count the numbers of my woes, and I will either move the thoughtless flint — make hard-as-flint Dido love me — or drop both of my eyes out in drizzling tears, before the course of my sorrow stops."

"I will not leave Iarbas, whom I love, in this delight of dying pensiveness," Anna said. "You are taking delight in swooning sorrow. Away with Dido! Let Anna be your song — Anna, who admires you more than heaven."

"I may not and will not listen to such a loathsome change — Anna for Dido! — that intercepts the course of my desire," Iarbus said brutally.

He called, "Servants, come fetch these empty vessels here, for I will flee from these alluring eyes of Anna that pursue my peace wherever it goes."

The vessels were empty because Anna had interrupted the sacrifice before Iarbas could slaughter the animal; the vessels were used to collect the animal's blood.

As Iarbas left, Anna called, "Iarbas, stay! Loving Iarbas, stay, for I have honey to present to you. Hard-hearted man, won't you hear me speak? I'll follow you with outcries nevertheless and strew your walks with my disheveled hair."

Alone, Aeneas talked to himself:

"Carthage, my friendly host, adieu, since destiny calls me from your shore. Hermes this night, descending in a dream, has summoned me to fruitful Italy. Jove wills it so. My mother wills it so. Let my Phoenissa — the Phoenician Elissa, aka Dido — grant me permission to leave, and then I go.

"Whether she grants me permission or not, Aeneas must go. My golden fortunes, clogged with courtly ease, cannot ascend to Fame's immortal house and cannot feast in bright Honor's burnished — polished — hall, until Aeneas has furrowed Neptune's glassy fields and cut a passage through his topless hills."

To reach Italy, Aeneas would have to sail the sea, which he likened here to plowing a field and making a journey through mountainous territory. In Italy, he would find his destiny.

Aeneas called, "Achates, come here! Sergestus, Ilioneus, Cloanthus, hasten away! Aeneas calls you."

Achates, Cloanthus, Ilioneus, and Sergestus came over to Aeneas.

"What does our lord want?" Achates asked. "Why is he calling us?"

Aeneas answered, "The dreams, brave mates, that did beset my bed when sleep but newly had embraced the night, command me to leave these unrenowned realms, where nobility abhors to stay, and none but base Aeneas will abide."

Carthage was not where Aeneas was fated to find renown, and so for Aeneas to choose to stay here would show that he is a base and not a noble man. Later, Carthage would compete with Rome to dominate the Mediterranean, but now Carthage was just being built, and Rome would not exist for hundreds of years.

Aeneas said to his Trojan companions, "Aboard, aboard, since Fates do bid us go on board and slice the sea with sable-colored ships — ships with black sails on which the nimble winds may all day attend, and follow them, as footmen, through the deep.

"Yet Dido casts her eyes like anchors out, to prevent my fleet from leaving the bay. 'Come back, come back,' I hear her cry from afar, 'and let me link your body to my lips, so that, tied together by the striving tongues, we may, as one, sail to Italy.'"

Achates said, "Banish that enticing dame from your mouth; don't let her kiss you. Instead, follow your foreseeing stars in everything. Follow the destiny that the stars that reigned at your birth prophesized. This life in Carthage is no life for men-at-arms to live — here romantic dalliance consumes a soldier's strength, and wanton motions of alluring eyes make our minds, which have been inured to war, effeminate."

"Why, let us build a city of our own, and not stand lingering here for amorous looks," Ilioneus said. "Will Dido raise old Priam out of his grave and rebuild the town the Greeks burned? No, no; she doesn't care whether we sink or swim, as long as she may have Aeneas in her arms."

"To Italy, sweet friends, to Italy!" Cloanthus said. "We will not stay here a minute longer."

"Trojans, go on board the ships, and I will follow you," Aeneas said.

Everyone except Aeneas exited.

He said to himself, "I gladly would go, yet beauty calls me back. To leave Dido so quickly like this and not once say farewell would be to transgress against all the laws of love, but if I use such ceremonious thanks and words that parting lovers are accustomed to say on the shore, her silver arms will embrace me round about my neck and shedding tears of pearl, she will cry, 'Stay, Aeneas, stay.' Each word she says will then contain a crown, and every speech will be ended with a kiss. I may not endure this female drudgery. I cannot endure being held in slavery by a woman, and I cannot endure these words, hugs, and kisses that Dido will give me if she finds out that I am leaving. Go to sea, Aeneas! Find Italy!"

Dido and Anna talked together in a room of her palace.

"Oh, Anna, run to the shore where Aeneas' ships are located," Dido said. "They say Aeneas' men are going on board. It may be he will steal away with them. Don't stay to answer me. Run, Anna, run."

Anna ran from the room.

Dido said to herself, "Oh, foolish Trojans who would steal away from here and not let Dido know ahead of time their intention of leaving. I would have given Achates a store of gold, and I would have given Ilioneus frankincense and Libyan spices. I would have given the common soldiers rich embroidered coats and silver whistles to control the winds, which the goddess Circe sent my late husband, Sichaeus, when he lived. They are unworthy of a Queen's reward."

Sailors used whistles to communicate during storms at sea.

Anna returned, bringing with her Aeneas, Achates, Ilioneus, and Sergestus.

Dido said to herself, "See where they come. How might I do to chide? Is criticizing Aeneas a good idea?"

"It was time for me to run," Anna said. "Aeneas would have been gone; the sails were being hoisted up and he was on board the ship."

Dido asked Aeneas, "Is this how you show your love to me?"

"Oh, princely Dido, give me permission to speak," Aeneas said. "I went to take my farewell of Achates."

Dido asked, "How does it happen that Achates did not tell me farewell?"

"Because I feared your grace would keep me here," Achates answered.

"To rid you of that fear," Dido said, "I tell you to go on board the ship again. I order you to go out to sea, and not stay here."

"Then let Aeneas go on board with us," Achates said.

"Get yourself on board," Dido said. "Aeneas intends to stay in Carthage."

"The sea is rough," Aeneas said. "The winds blow to the shore."

"Oh, false Aeneas!" Dido said. "Now the sea is rough, but when you were on board, the sea was calm enough. You and Achates meant to sail away."

"Haven't you, the Queen of Carthage, my only son?" Aeneas asked. "Do you, Dido, think I will go and leave him here?"

Aeneas made a good point. He had not left his son behind at Troy and was unlikely to do so in Carthage. It is possible, however, that he had recognized the disguised Cupid and realized that his son was somewhere safe and that Venus, his goddess mother, would later safely return his son to him.

Also, Anna may have misinterpreted what she had seen when she thought that Aeneas was ready to sail away from Carthage.

Of course, Aeneas had made up his mind to leave Carthage, but he had also at least seriously considered telling Dido that he was leaving.

"Aeneas, pardon me, for I forgot that young Ascanius slept in my bed last night," Dido said.

She continued, "Love made me jealous, but to make amends, wear the imperial crown of Libya. Hold the Punic scepter in my stead, and punish me, Aeneas, for this crime."

"This kiss shall be fair Dido's punishment," Aeneas said, kissing her.

She put the crown on his head and put the scepter in his hand.

"Oh, how a crown becomes Aeneas' head," Dido said. "Stay here, Aeneas, and command as King of Carthage."

"How vain would I be to wear this diadem and bear this golden scepter in my hand," Aeneas said. "A helmet of steel and not a crown, a sword and not a scepter are suitable for Aeneas."

"Oh, keep them always, and let me gaze my fill," Dido said. "Now Aeneas looks like immortal Jove. Oh, where are Ganymede to hold his cup and Mercury to fly and get what he calls for? May ten thousand Cupids hover in the air and fan Aeneas' lovely face.

"Oh, I wish that the clouds were here, wherein you flee, so that you and I unseen might sport ourselves."

During the Trojan War, Jupiter wrapped clouds around Juno and himself so that no one could see them making love on Mount Ida. Dido wanted this to happen to Aeneas and her. By spending his time having sex with Dido, Aeneas would be fleeing his destiny in Italy.

Treacherous Juno had slept with Jupiter to trick him into not paying attention to the Trojan War so that the Greeks could rally against the Trojans, who were fighting well. In her own more innocent way, Dido was treacherous to Aeneas because she was keeping him from pursuing his destiny.

Dido continued, "Heaven, envious of our joys, has grown pale, and when we whisper, then the stars fall down to be partakers of our honey talk."

"Oh, Dido, patroness of all our lives, when I leave you, may death be my punishment," Aeneas said. "Swell, raging seas. Frown, wayward destinies. Blow, winds. Threaten, rocks and sandbars. This is the harbor that Aeneas seeks. Let's see what harm tempests can bring to me now."

"Not all the world can take you from my arms," Dido said. "Aeneas may command as many African moors as in the sea are little waterdrops, and now, to demonstrate my love for Aeneas, fair sister Anna, lead my lover forth and, with him seated on my horse, let him ride as Dido's husband through the Punic — Carthaginian — streets, and order my guard with Mauritanian spears to wait upon him as their sovereign lord."

"What if the citizens complain at this?" Anna asked.

"Command my guard to slay for their offense those who dislike what Dido orders," Dido replied. "Shall vulgar peasants storm at what I do? The ground is mine that gives them sustenance. The air that they breathe, the water, fire, all that they have, their lands, their goods, and their lives are mine. And I, the goddess of all these, command that Aeneas shall ride as the King of Carthage."

Achates said, "Aeneas, because of his parentage, deserves as large a kingdom as is Libya."

"Yes, and unless the Destinies — the Fates — are false, I shall be planted in as rich a land," Aeneas said.

He may have been referring to Italy.

"Speak of no other land," Dido said. "This land is yours. Dido is yours; henceforth I'll call you lord."

In this society, wives called their husbands lord.

Dido ordered Anna, "Do what I order you to do, sister. Lead the way, and from a turret I'll behold my love."

"Then here in me shall flourish Priam's race," Aeneas said. "And you and I, Achates, for revenge for Troy, for Priam, for his fifty sons, our kinsmen's lives, and a thousand guiltless souls, will lead an army against the hateful Greeks and set on fire proud Sparta of Lacedaemon over their heads."

Everyone exited except Dido and a Carthaginian lord.

"Doesn't Aeneas speak like a conqueror?" she said. "Oh, blessed tempests that drove him to Carthage! Oh, happy sand that made him run aground here! Henceforth you shall be our Carthage gods.

"Yes, but it may be he will leave my love and seek a foreign land called Italy. Oh, I wish that I had a charm to keep the winds enclosed within a golden ball, or that the Mediterranean Sea were in my arms, so that he might suffer shipwreck on my breast as often as he attempts to hoist up sail.

"I must anticipate what he will do and stop him from leaving. Wishing will not serve."

She commanded, "Go and order my nurse to take young Ascanius and carry him to her house in the country. Aeneas will not leave without his son.

"Yet, lest he should leave without his son, for I am full of fear, bring me his oars, his tackling, and his sails."

The Carthaginian lord exited.

Dido said to herself, "What if I sink his ships? Oh, he'll frown. Better he should frown than I should die for grief.

"But I cannot see him frown; it may not be. Armies of foes resolved to conquer this town, or impious traitors vowed to murder me and have my life, do not frighten me; only Aeneas' frown is that which terrifies poor Dido's heart.

"Not bloody spears, appearing in the air, that presage the downfall of my sovereignty, nor threatening blazing comets that foretell Dido's death, but only Aeneas' frown will end my days.

"If he does not forsake me, I will never die, for in his looks I see eternity, and he'll make me immortal with a kiss."

The Carthaginian lord returned, accompanied by some attendants carrying tackling, oars, and sails.

"Your nurse has left with young Ascanius," the Carthaginian lord said, "and here's Aeneas' tackling, oars, and sails."

"Are these the sails that, in despite of me, maliciously conspired with the winds to bear Aeneas away from Carthage?" Dido said. "I'll hang you sails in the chamber where I lie. Drive if you can my house to Italy. I'll set the window open, so that the winds may enter in and once again conspire against the life of me, poor Queen of Carthage. But although you blow my house to Italy, Aeneas will still be in Carthage because he will still be in my house. So let rich Carthage float upon the seas, as long as I may have Aeneas in my arms."

Looking at the wooden oars, she said, "Is this the wood that grew on Carthaginian plains, and would be toiling in the watery billows to rob their mistress of her Trojan guest? Oh, cursed tree, if you only had the intelligence or sense to measure how much I prize Aeneas' love, you would have leaped from out of the sailors' hands and told me that Aeneas meant to go. And yet I don't blame you; you are only wood.

"The water, which our poets call in poems a nymph, why did it allow you oars to touch her breast and did not shrink back, knowing my love was there in the ship? The water is an element, no nymph.

"Why should I blame Aeneas for his flight? Oh, Dido, don't blame him, but break his oars. These were the instruments that launched him forth.

"There's not so much as this base tackling, too, but dares to heap up sorrow to my heart. Wasn't it you, the tackling, that hoisted up these sails? Why didn't you ropes break so that the sails fell in the seas? Because you did not break, Dido will tie you ropes full of knots and cut you all asunder with her hands. Then you will be used to chastise shipboys for their faults — you will be used to flog sailors. No more will you offend me, the Carthaginian Queen.

"Now let him hang my favors — my ribbons — on his masts and see if those will serve instead of sails.

"As for tackling, let him take the chains of gold that I bestowed upon his followers.

"Instead of oars, let him use his hands and swim to Italy.

"I'll keep these sails, oars, and tackling somewhere secure where Aeneas cannot get them."

She ordered, "Come, carry them in."

The nurse talked to Cupid, who was still disguised as Ascanius.

"My lord Ascanius, you must go with me."

"Where must I go?" the disguised Cupid said. "I'll stay with my mother."

By "mother," he meant Queen Dido.

"No, you shall go with me to my house," the nurse said. "I have an orchard that has lots of plums, brown almonds, pears, ripe figs, and dates, blackberries and gooseberries, apples, yellow oranges, a garden where are beehives full of honey, musk roses, and a thousand kinds of flowers, and in the midst runs a silver stream, where you shall see the red-gilled fishes leap, white swans, and many lovely waterfowl. Now speak, Ascanius, will you go or not?"

"Come, come, I'll go," the disguised Cupid said. "How far from here is your house?"

"It's nearby," the nurse said. "We shall get there quickly."

"Nurse, I am weary," the disguised Cupid said. "Will you carry me?"

"Yes, as long as you'll dwell with me and call me mother."

"As long as you'll love me, I don't care if I do," the disguised Cupid said.

The nurse picked him up; being so close to and touching the god of love affected her thoughts, turning them toward love.

"I wish that I might live to see this boy become a man!" the nurse said. "How prettily he laughs. Go on, you mischievous boy! You'll be a ladies' man when you come of age."

Because Cupid was mischievous, he kept inflaming the nurse's sexual desire and then putting it out.

The nurse said, "Let Dido say what she will, I am not old. I'll be no more a widow. I am young; I'll have a husband, or else a lover."

The disguised Cupid said, "A husband, and no teeth?"

The nurse said, "Oh, what do I mean to have such foolish thoughts! Love is foolish, just a foolish toy.

"Oh, sacred love! If there be any heaven in earth, it is love. Especially in women of my years.

"Blush, blush for shame! Why should you think of love? A grave, and not a lover, befits your age.

"A grave? Why? I may live a hundred years; fourscore — eighty — is just a girl's age. Love is sweet.

"My veins are withered and my sinews dry. Why do I think of love, now I should die?"

"Come, nurse," the disguised Cupid said.

Thinking of a former suitor, the nurse said, "Well, if he come a wooing, he shall speed and succeed. Oh, how unwise I was to say no to him!"

CHAPTER 5
— 5.1 —

Aeneas drew on a piece of paper the layout of Carthage. With him were Achates, Cloanthus, Ilioneus, and Sergestus.

"Triumph, my mates," Aeneas said. "Our travels are at an end. Here Aeneas will build a statelier Troy than that which grim Atrides — Agamemnon, the son of Atreus — overthrew.

"Carthage shall boast petty walls no more, for I will grace them with a fairer frame and clad her in a crystal livery wherein the day may forevermore delight. I will build higher walls made of glittering crystals.

"From golden India I will fetch the Ganges River, whose wealthy streams may wait upon the towers of Carthage and with three moats entrench her round about.

"The sun shall bring rich odors from Egypt. The sun's burning beams, like laboring bees that load their thighs with honey from Hybla, shall here unburden their exhaled sweet scents and plant our pleasant suburbs with their fumes. Yes, the sun shall inhale sweet scents from Egypt and then exhale them here in Carthage."

"What length or width shall this brave town contain?" Achates asked.

"Not past four thousand paces square at the most," Aeneas said.

"But what shall it be called?" Ilioneus asked. "Troy, as before?"

"I haven't decided on a name yet," Aeneas replied.

"Let it be called Aenea, after your name," Cloanthus said.

"Rather, call it Ascania, after your little son," Sergestus said.

"No, I will have it called Anchisaeon," Aeneas said, "after the name of my old father: Anchises."

Hermes arrived with the real Ascanius.

"Aeneas, wait!" Hermes said. "Jove's herald tells you to wait."

Jupiter did not want Aeneas to build the walls of Carthage; Aeneas' destiny was different.

"Whom do I see?" Aeneas said. "Jove's winged messenger? Welcome to Carthage, this newly erected town."

Both Aeneas and Hermes were related: Both Aeneas and Hermes could trace their ancestry back to Jupiter.

"Why, kinsman," Hermes said, "do you stand building cities here and beautifying the empire of this Queen Dido, while Italy is clean out of your mind? You are too, too forgetful of your own affairs. Why will you so betray your son's good destiny?"

Not only was Aeneas ignoring his own destiny in Italy, but he also was ignoring his son's destiny in Italy.

Hermes continued, "Jupiter, the King of gods, sent me from highest heaven to sound this angry message in your ears: Vain man, what monarchy do you expect to have here, and with what thought do you sleep on the shore of Libya? If you have forsaken all thought of and you despise the praise of such undertakings, yet think upon Ascanius' prophecy, and young Iulus' more than a thousand years of empire."

Another name for Ascanius was Iulus, from which the name Julius, as in Julius Caesar, derived. Ascanius was destined to found the town of Alba Longa in Italy, and from him would descend many Kings. Romulus and Remus would then found the city of Rome, and the Roman Empire and the Byzantine Empire (the eastern half of the Roman Empire) would last more than a thousand years.

Hermes continued, "I have brought Ascanius from the Idalian groves where he slept, and I carried young Cupid to the island of Cyprus."

Aeneas immediately knew, if he had not known earlier, what had happened: "This was my mother who beguiled the Queen of Carthage and made me mis-take my half-brother, Cupid, for my son. It is no marvel, Dido, that you are in love with me because daily you dandled Cupid in your arms."

This is an additional reason for Aeneas to leave Queen Dido and Carthage and go to Italy. Dido's love for him is not real love: Venus and Cupid made her love Aeneas. Dido had no choice: She did not fall in love of her own free will.

"Welcome, sweet child," Aeneas said to his son. "Where have you been this long while?"

"Eating sweets with Queen Dido's maid," Ascanius replied, "who ever since has lulled me in her arms."

Apparently, Hermes went to the nurse's house and substituted Ascanius for Cupid, flew Cupid to Cyprus, and then returned to take Ascanius to Aeneas.

"Sergestus, bear Ascanius to our ships," Aeneas ordered, "lest Dido, spying him, keep him for a hostage."

Sergestus exited with Ascanius.

Hermes said, "Do you spend your time thinking about this little boy, and do not think about Jove's order I bring you? I tell you that you must sail immediately to Italy, or else endure the wrath of frowning Jove."

Hermes exited.

Aeneas asked, "How can I set sail into the raging deep, when I have no sails or tackling for my ships? Would the gods have me, like Deucalion, float up and down wherever the billows drive?"

When Jupiter decided to cause a great flood, he allowed Deucalion and his wife, Pyrrha, to survive on an ark Deucalion built.

Aeneas continued, "Although Dido repaired my fleet and gave me ships, yet she has taken away my oars and masts, and left me neither sail nor rudder on board."

Iarbas arrived and asked, "How are you now, Aeneas? Sad? What is the meaning of your sad mood?"

"Iarbas, I am entirely beside myself," Aeneas said. "Jove has heaped upon me such a desperate charge, which neither skill nor reason may achieve, nor can I devise by what means to contrive to carry out what Jove has ordered me to do."

"What have you been ordered to do, may I ask?" Iarbus said. "May I persuade you to tell me?"

"Jove orders me to speedily sail to Italy," Aeneas said, "but I lack both rigging for my fleet and equipment for my men."

"If that is all, then cheer up your drooping looks, for I will furnish you with such supplies," Iarbus said. "Let some of your followers go with me, and they shall have whatsoever things you need."

Iarbus was happy to help Aeneas, his rival for Dido's love, leave Carthage and sail to Italy.

"Thanks, good Iarbas, for your friendly aid," Aeneas said. "Achates and the rest shall wait on you and gather the equipment, while I rest thankful for this courtesy."

Iarbas and Aeneas' companions exited.

Aeneas said to himself, "Now I will hasten to the Lavinian shore in Italy and raise a new foundation to old Troy. But let the gods witness, and let heaven and earth witness, how loath I am to leave this Libyan territory, but I must because immortal Jupiter commands me to."

Dido, accompanied by attendants, entered the scene and walked over to Aeneas.

She said to herself, "I fear I saw Aeneas' little son being led by Achates to the Trojan fleet. If it is so, his father means to flee from Carthage to Italy. But here he is. Now, Dido, use your intelligence in talking to Aeneas."

She wanted to persuade him to stay in Carthage.

Dido said out loud, "Aeneas, why do your men go on board the ships? Why are your ships newly rigged? For what purpose, launched from the haven, do the ships float in the calm water? Pardon me, though I ask you. Love makes me ask."

"Oh, pardon me if I tell you why," Aeneas said. "Aeneas will not lie to his dear love: I must go away from here. This day, when I was laying a platform for these walls, swift Mercury, sent from Jove, his father, appeared to me, and in his father's name rebuked me bitterly for lingering here, neglecting Italy."

"But yet Aeneas will not leave his love," Dido said.

"I am commanded by immortal Jove to leave this town and journey to Italy, and therefore I must obey," Aeneas said.

"These words don't come from Aeneas' heart," Dido said.

"Not from my heart, for I can hardly go," Aeneas said. "Leaving you is difficult, and yet I may not stay. Dido, farewell."

"'Farewell?' Is this the amends for Dido's love?" Dido said. "Are Trojans accustomed to leave their lovers like that? Dido may fare well, as long as Aeneas stays. I will die if my Aeneas says farewell."

"Then let me go and never say farewell," Aeneas said.

"'Let me go'! 'Farewell'! 'I must leave'! These words are poison to poor Dido's soul," Dido said. "Oh, speak like my Aeneas, like my love. Why do you look toward the sea? The time has been when Dido's beauty chained your eyes to her. Am I less beautiful than when you first saw me? Oh, if I am not, Aeneas, then it is out of grief for you. Say that you will stay in Carthage with your Queen, and Dido's beauty will return again.

"Aeneas, say how you can take your leave. Will you kiss Dido?"

She kissed him.

Dido continued, "Oh, your lips have sworn to stay with Dido! Can you take her hand?"

She held his hand.

Dido continued, "Your hand and mine have plighted mutual faith.

"Therefore, unkind Aeneas, must you say, 'Then let me go, and never say farewell'?"

"Oh, Queen of Carthage, even if you were ugly and black," Aeneas said, "Aeneas could not choose but hold you dear."

This society regarded black complexions as ugly.

Aeneas continued, "Yet Aeneas must not gainsay the gods' behest. I must obey the gods' orders."

"The gods?" Dido asked. "What gods are those who seek my death? In what have I offended Jupiter that he should take Aeneas from my arms? Oh, no! The gods don't care what lovers do. It is Aeneas who calls Aeneas away from here, and woeful Dido, by these blubbered cheeks, by this right hand, and by our spousal rites, desires Aeneas to remain with her."

She then said in Latin:

"Si bene quid de te merui, fuit aut tibi quidquam

"Dulce meum, miserere domus labentis, et istam,

"Oro, si quis adhuc precibus locus, exue mentem."

These are lines 317-319 from Book IV of Virgil's *Aeneid*.

Translated:

"If you owe me anything, if anything in me

"Ever pleased you, take pity on my fallen fortunes and our fallen house [— the family we made together]!

"If prayer is still possible, I pray that you will change your mind."

Aeneas replied in Latin:

"Desine meque tuis incendere teque querelis;

"Italiam non sponte sequor."

These are lines 360-361 from Book IV of Virgil's *Aeneid*.

Translated:

"Stop upsetting yourself, and me, with these complaints.

"I do not seek Italy of my own free will."

Dido replied, "Have you forgotten how many neighboring Kings were up in arms because I made you my love? How the citizens of Carthage did rebel, Iarbas storm, and all the world call me a second Helen of Troy — a whore — for being entangled by a foreigner's looks?

"As long as you would prove to be as true to me as Paris did to Helen, I would wish, as fair Troy was, that Carthage might be sacked, and I be called a second Helen.

"If I had a son by you, my grief would be less because I could see you, Aeneas, in our son's face. Now, if you go, what can you leave behind except that which will augment rather than ease my woe?"

"In vain, my love, you spend your fainting breath," Aeneas said. "If words could move me, I would have already been overcome by your words."

"And won't you be moved with Dido's words?" Dido said. "Your mother was no goddess, perjured man, nor was Dardanus the author of your stock — he is no ancestor of yours. But instead you are sprung from the Scythian Caucasus mountain range — you are hard-hearted — and the tigers of Hyrcania nursed you when you were a baby.

"Ah, foolish Dido, to endure this long!

"Weren't you wrecked upon this Libyan shore, and didn't you come to me, Dido, like a peasant fisherman? Didn't I repair your ships, make you a King, and make all your needy followers noblemen?

"Oh, you serpent that came creeping from the shore and I out of pity harbored you in my bosom, will you now slay me with your poisonous fangs and hiss at Dido for preserving you?

"Go, go, and spare not. Seek out Italy. I hope that that which love forbids me to do — destroy your fleet — the rocks and sea-gulfs will fully perform, and you shall perish in the billowing waves to which poor Dido bequeaths revenge.

"Yes, traitor, and the waves shall cast you up on shore where you and treacherous Achates first set foot.

"If that happens, I'll give you burial and weep upon your lifeless carcasses, although neither you nor he will pity me now even a whit.

"Why do you stare at my face? If you will stay, leap into my arms. My arms are open wide. If you will not stay, turn away from me, and I'll turn away from you, for although you have the heart to say farewell, I have not the power to stop you and keep you here."

Aeneas exited.

"Is he gone?" Dido said to herself. "Yes, but he'll come again. He cannot go. He loves me too, too well to treat me so. Yet he who in my sight would not relent will, being absent from my sight, continue to be obdurate."

She engaged in wishful imagining:

"By this time he has gotten to the shore, and, see, the sailors take him by the hand, but he shrinks back, and now, remembering me, returns as quickly as he can. Welcome, welcome, my love!"

She returned to reality: "But where's Aeneas? Ah, he's gone, he's gone!"

Anna entered and asked, "Why does my sister rave and cry like this?"

"Oh, Anna, my Aeneas is on board ship, and leaving me, he will sail to Italy. Once you went after him, and he came back again. Now bring him back, and you shall be a Queen, and I will live a private life with him."

"Wicked Aeneas!" Anna said.

"Don't call him wicked, sister. Speak well about him, and look upon him with a mermaid's eye."

Mermaids often admire sailors.

Dido continued, "Tell him, I never vowed at Aulis' gulf the desolation of his native Troy, nor sent a thousand ships unto the walls, nor ever violated faith and was disloyal to him."

Aulis is the port in Greece where the Greek ships met before crossing the Mediterranean Sea to attack and conquer Troy.

Dido continued, "Request him gently, Anna, to return. I crave only this: He will stay a tide or two, so that I may learn to bear his departure patiently. If he will depart thus suddenly, I die. Run, Anna, run. Don't stay to answer me."

As she left, Anna said, "I go, fair sister. May the heavens grant us good success."

Anna exited, and the nurse entered.

"Oh, Dido, your little son — Ascanius — is gone," the nurse said. "He slept in my bed with me last night, and in the morning I discovered that he was stolen from me. I think some fairies have tricked me."

"Oh, cursed hag and treacherous, lying wretch," Dido said, "you kill me with your harsh and hellish tale. You for some petty gift — some bribe — have let him go, and I am thus deprived and defrauded of my boy."

She ordered, "Take the nurse away to prison immediately."

She then said to the nurse, "You are a traitoress, a too keenly cruel and cursed sorceress!"

"I don't know what you mean by treason, I don't," the nurse said. "I am as true as any other servant of yours."

"Away with her," Dido ordered. "Don't allow her to speak."

An attendant took the nurse away.

Dido looked up and said, "My sister is coming. I don't like her sad looks."

Anna entered and said, "Before I arrived at the harbor, Aeneas was already on board the ship, and, seeing me, he ordered the sailors to quickly hoist up the sails. But I cried out, 'Aeneas, false Aeneas, wait!' Then he began to wave his hand, which because he continued to hold it up, made me suppose he would have heard me speak."

Anna may have been mistaken: The waving of his hand may have been part of Aeneas' giving orders to his men.

She continued, "Then they began to drive into the ocean, which when I viewed it, I cried, 'Aeneas, stay! Dido, fair Dido, wants Aeneas to stay!' Yet my tears and laments could not mollify a whit his heart of hard adamant or flint.

"Then heedlessly I tore out my hair for grief, which being seen by all the sailors, although he, having turned his back on me, did not see me doing it, they began to try to persuade him to remedy my grief and stay a while to hear what I could say, but he, imprisoning himself below deck, sailed away."

Anna may have been mistaken: The sailors may have been advising Aeneas to go below the deck.

"Oh, Anna, Anna, I will follow him," Dido said.

"How can you go after him, when he has all your fleet?" Anna asked.

"I'll make myself wings of wax like those of Icarus, and over his ships I will soar close to the sun, so that the wax of my wings will melt and I will fall into his arms."

Daedalus and his son, Icarus, were imprisoned on Crete. To escape, Daedalus made wings for himself and his son from wax and feathers. He warned his son not to fly too close to the sun, but impetuous Icarus did. The wax of his wings melted, the feathers fell out, and Icarus fell into the sea and drowned.

Dido continued, "Or else I'll make a prayer to the waves so that I may swim to him like Triton's niece."

Dido was mixing up mythological stories. Two Scyllas existed. The Scylla who was related to the sea-god Triton was a monster that devoured some of Ulysses' men as he returned home from Troy. The other Scylla was the daughter of King Nisus of Megara. She fell in love with King Minos of Crete, and when he sailed away from Megara, she attempted to swim after him but drowned.

Dido continued, "Oh, Anna, fetch Arion's harp so that I may entice a dolphin to the shore and ride upon its back to my love."

According to legend, Arion, a skilled musician, was on a ship that pirates captured. The pirates were going to force him to commit suicide, and Arion requested the boon of playing one last song. After playing the song, he jumped into the sea, but a music-loving dolphin brought him to shore.

Dido now began imagining things:

"Look, sister, look! Lovely Aeneas' ships! See, see, the billows heave him up to heaven, and now down fall the keels into the deep. Oh, sister, sister, take away the rocks. They'll break his ships. Oh, Proteus,

Neptune, Jove, save, save Aeneas, Dido's dearest love. Now he has come on shore, safe without hurt. But see, Achates wants him to put to sea, and all the sailors make merry for joy. But Aeneas, remembering me, shrinks back again. See, he comes! Welcome, welcome, my love!"

"Ah, sister," Anna said, "leave these idle fantasies. Sweet sister, stop. Remember who you are."

"I am Dido, unless I am deceived," Dido said. "And must I rave like this for a runaway who renounces his vows? Must I make ships for him to sail away? Nothing can bear me to him but a ship, and he has all my fleet."

She thought, *What shall I do but die in fury at this oversight? Yes, I must be the murderer of myself. No, but I am not; yet I will be very quickly.*

Dido said out loud, "Anna, be glad. Now I have found a means by which to rid me of these thoughts of lunacy. Not far from here is a woman who is famous for the occult arts and daughter to the nymphs called Hesperides, who are the guardians of the golden apples. This woman wants me to sacrifice Aeneas' enticing relics — the things he left behind.

"Go, Anna, tell my servants to bring me fire."

Anna exited, and Iarbas entered.

Iarbus asked, "How long will Dido mourn the flight of a foreigner who has dishonored both her and Carthage? How long shall I with grief consume my days, and reap no reward for my truest love?"

Some attendants entered, carrying wood and lit torches. They put down the items and then left.

"Iarbas," Dido said, "don't talk about Aeneas; let him go. Work with your hands, and help me make a fire that shall consume all that this foreigner left behind, for I intend to perform a private sacrifice that will cure my mind that melts for unkind love."

"But afterwards," Iarbus asked, "will Dido grant me love?"

"Yes, yes, Iarbas," Dido said. "After this is done, none in the world shall have my love but you."

They made a fire, and Dido said, "So! Leave me now. Let none approach this place."

Iarbas exited.

Alone, Dido said, "Now, Dido, with these relics burn yourself, and make Aeneas famous throughout the world for perjury and the slaughter of a Queen."

She began putting Aeneas' relics into the fire as she said, "Here let lie the sword that in the dark cave he drew and swore by to be true to me. You shall burn first; your crime is worse than his.

"Here let lie the garment that I clothed him in when first he came on shore. Perish, too.

"These letters, lines, and perjured papers all shall burn to cinders in this precious flame."

Having put the relics in the fire, she said, "And now, you gods who guide the starry universe and order all things at your high bestowal, grant, although the traitors land in Italy, that they may be still tormented with unrest. And from my ashes let a conqueror rise who may revenge this treason to a Queen by plowing up Aeneas' countries with the sword. Between this land and that land of his let there never be peace."

Later ages would say that the conqueror Dido called up was Hannibal, a Carthaginian general who warred against Rome and spent many years in Italy with an army hostile to Rome.

Dido said in Latin:

"*Litora litoribus contraria, fluctibus undas*

"*Imprecor, arma armis; pugnent ipsique nepotes.*"

Translated:

"Let your shores oppose their shores, let your waves oppose their waves, let your weapons oppose their weapons. That is my curse. Let them fight — they, and their sons' sons, forever."

Dido continued, "Live, false Aeneas! Truest Dido dies!"

She said in Latin:

"*Sic, sic juvat ire sub umbras.*"

Translated:

"Thus, thus I am pleased to go into the shadows."

Dido threw herself into the flames.

Anna entered, saw what had happened, and screamed, "Oh, help, Iarbas! Dido in these flames has burnt herself. Ah, me! Unhappy me!"

Iarbas, running, entered the room and said, "Cursed Iarbas, die to extinguish the grief that tears at your inward soul. Dido, I am coming to you. Ah, me, Aeneas!"

He jumped into the fire.

Anna said, "How can my tears or cries help me now? Dido is dead, Iarbas is slain. Iarbas, my dear love! Oh, sweet Iarbas, Anna's sole delight. What fatal destiny hates me thus, to see my sweet Iarbas slay himself? But Anna now shall honor you in death and mix her blood with yours. This shall I do, so that gods and men may pity my death and bitterly regret our ends, senseless and without life or breath.

"Now, sweet Iarbas, wait for me! I am coming to you!"

She jumped into the fire.

APPENDIX A: BOOK 4 OF VIRGIL'S AENEID

The Passion of Dido

But the queen, Dido, was now seriously in love. Aeneas' story had been of the many dangers he had faced and survived. His story had also been of his heroism, including going back into a burning city filled with enemy warriors so he could search for his missing wife. His story was pleasing to unmarried Dido.

Dido's love for Aeneas gave her no rest, no peace. Her love burned.

As dawn arrived, Dido, who had not been able to sleep, said to Anna, her sister, "I am impressed by this stranger, this Aeneas. He is noble, he is courageous, and he is a mighty warrior. He must be the son of a god. A lowborn man would have shown fear amid the many dangers he has faced. The story he told us is impressive.

"When my husband died, I vowed to myself and to his ashes that I would not remarry. I had married one man, and my heart broke when he died. If not for this vow, I would be tempted to marry Aeneas. My own brother murdered my husband and spilled his blood and angered our household gods. Ever since then, Aeneas is the only man I have been interested in. For my husband, I felt the flame of love. When I think of Aeneas, and I think of him all the time, I feel again the flame of love.

"But I think it is best if I die before I break the vow that I have made not to remarry. I want to be true to my vow. I want to be true to my conscience. Queens and well-born women should not have affairs."

Dido stopped speaking. She cried.

Anna replied, "Why shouldn't you be remarried? Why shouldn't you know the joys of children of your own? Why shouldn't you know once more the joys of love? Will the ashes and ghosts of the dead care that you remarry? A city needs a king, not just a queen. The leader of a city must leave behind children who will grow up and assume power.

"You can do what you wish, but no one has tempted you to remarry before this. Back in Tyre, the city that we fled, and here in Libya, the land that we fled to, no one has tempted you to remarry before this. You have had suitors. Iarbas of Libya wanted to marry you, but you turned him down. Other suitors in Libya have courted you.

"But now that you are in love, why resist your love?

"Think of Carthage. What would be best for your people? Not all of our neighbors are friendly. On one side are dangerous peoples, including the wild Numidians. On the other side are a dangerous desert and a dangerous people: the raiders of Barce. Remember also that your brother is dangerous; he may make war on you from Tyre. Carthage needs a king who can lead troops into war when necessary.

"Juno has shown the Carthaginians great favor, I think, by sending the Trojan ships here.

"If you marry Aeneas, Carthage will have an impressive king. If the Carthaginian warriors and the Trojan warriors join together, think what an army we will have! We will have a mighty city and a mighty kingdom!

"As for the vow you made to yourself and to your late husband's ashes, pray to the gods. Sacrifice to them. Win them over.

"And keep our Trojan guests here. Winter is coming, and the Trojan ships are now too battered from the storm to sail. You have good reasons to use to convince Aeneas to stay here. Treat him and the Trojans like kings so that they will want to stay."

Anna's words helped convince Dido to hope for love, to break her vow, and to not worry about shame.

Dido and Anna visited several altars, and at each altar they sacrificed to the gods — to Ceres, Apollo, Bacchus, and Juno. They especially sacrificed to and prayed to Juno, the goddess of marriage.

Dido poured wine over the horns of a white cow and other sacrificial victims, and after the victims were killed, she examined their entrails for signs from the gods.

But Dido was in love, and her love was like a wound. She wandered the streets of the city. She was like a deer that an archer shoots in the forests of Crete. The archer is unaware that he has made a direct hit as the deer flees with the arrow in her side that will kill her.

Dido showed Aeneas the glories of Carthage. She wanted to tell him of her love for him, but her voice would not allow her to speak. She stopped in the middle of a sentence. Each night, she provided a feast for him and listened to his stories, wanting often to hear about the fall of Troy.

Whenever Aeneas and her guests left the feast, Dido sat in the chair he had vacated.

Dido was lost in love. She thought about Aeneas constantly, seeing and hearing him even when he was not present. Dido often held Ascanius in her lap, taking pleasure in his resemblance to his father.

Because Dido was in love, she no longer did her duty as ruler of Carthage. Before Aeneas came to Carthage, she had busied herself with the construction of her city. Only partially built, the city lay exposed to enemies. No longer did the Carthaginians build the walls and other fortifications. Work on the harbor was also only partially completed. Dido had given in to the *furor* of passionate love; she neglected her *pietas* of building and ruling a city.

Juno kept watch; she saw that Dido was in love. Dido was willing to sacrifice her pride and her reputation if she could have an affair with Aeneas.

Having formed a plot in her mind, Juno said to Venus, "You and your son Cupid have triumphed over Dido! You two have made her fall in love with Aeneas. You are the goddess of sexual passion, and Cupid is the god of love. Dido did not have a chance against you two.

"I know that you have not liked the rising walls of Carthage, a city I love, but why should you and I disagree? What good is it for we two goddesses to be opposed to each other?

"Here is a way for us to be at peace with each other. Why not allow Aeneas and Dido to be married? You are the one who made Dido fall in love with Aeneas, so I don't see why you would be opposed to their marriage. Aeneas, who is your favorite, and Dido can rule the Carthaginians together. Since Aeneas, your favorite, is the male, he will have the most power."

Venus knew that Juno had proposed a trick: a way for future Roman power to become future Carthaginian power. After all, if Aeneas never reached Latium and never founded his city, he could not found the Roman people and so the great power of the Roman people would never exist. Instead of Rome being the great power in the Mediterranean, Carthage would be the great power.

But Venus had her own secret plans. If Aeneas and Dido were to have an affair for a while, this would ensure that Aeneas would continue to receive the help he needed until he could set sail once more for Italy.

And so Venus said to Juno, "Your offer is a good offer, and I will not shun it. But will Jupiter agree that one city — Carthage — should be home to the exiles from Tyre *and* the exiles from Troy? I think that the Fates may forbid that. But you are the wife of Jupiter, and you have influence over him, so I will do what you say."

Juno replied, "I shall arrange everything. Let me tell you my plan. Tomorrow, Aeneas and Dido will go hunting together. I will create a storm. Everyone will scatter to seek shelter, and Aeneas and Dido will seek shelter in the same cave. I will be there. I will ensure that two will become one. This will be the marriage of Aeneas and Dido."

Venus nodded her consent to Juno's plan although she knew that the plan was meant to be a trap.

When dawn arrived, Carthaginians and Trojans prepared for the hunt. Huntsmen brought nets and spears. They brought horses and hunting dogs. Dido kept them waiting as she dressed. Finally, she appeared in rich clothing and with her hair neatly styled.

Now the Carthaginians and the Trojans were ready to hunt. Aeneas took the lead; his son, Ascanius, was with him. So were many, many hunters.

Following winter, Apollo visits the island of Delos to enjoy a festival, and around his altars dance people who worship him. Apollo swiftly goes to Delos as drums pound a welcome for him. As swiftly as Apollo goes to Delos, Aeneas went to the hunt.

The hunters found game: goats and deer. Ascanius rode his horse in the lead, but he longed for more dangerous game than goats and deer; he hoped to find a wild boar or a lion.

Before the hunters could find more dangerous game, a storm hurled hail at them. All scattered and sought shelter. Dido and Aeneas found and entered the same cave. Here the goddesses Earth and Juno lit what resembled wedding torches. Here nymphs sang what resembled a wedding song. Here the sky witnessed what resembled a wedding. But although Juno provided the trappings of a wedding, this was not a legal wedding. Aeneas did not hold the torch that a groom holds in a real marriage. Aeneas did not make the vows that a groom makes in a real marriage.

Dido called her relationship with Aeneas a marriage, but it was really an affair. Dido used the word "marriage" to lessen her feeling of guilt.

Rumors of the affair spread quickly to all the cities of Libya. Evil moves quickly, and of all evils, rumor moves the quickest. Rumor is the daughter of Mother Earth, who bore her after Jupiter had killed two of her sons: the Titan Coeus and the Giant Enceladus. Mother Earth gave birth to Rumor as a way to get revenge for the death of these sons.

Rumor has wings and many feathers. Her many eyes never sleep, and she has many tongues and many ears. By night she flies, and by day she watches and listens. She values lies as much as she values truths.

Now Rumor quickly travelled throughout Libya and filled the ears of Libyans. Rumor told all, "Aeneas, a Trojan, and Dido, Queen of Carthage, are having an affair. They neglect their duties because they are spending so much time having sex."

Rumor spread this gossip to many Libyans, and then she went to Iarbas, whom Dido had earlier declined to marry. Iarbas was the product of rape. Jupiter had raped a nymph in Libya, and she had given birth to a son: Iarbas. Jupiter suffered no punishment for his crime; as king of gods and men, he is too powerful to suffer punishment even for his many rapes. In contrast, mortals can be punished even for consensual love affairs.

Iarbas had built many temples and many altars to his father. He made sure that the sacred fires were kept burning. He made sure that the blood of many sacrificial animals reddened the ground. He made sure that wreathes of flowers decorated the doors of temples.

Maddened by rumor, Iarbas went to one of Jupiter's altars and prayed, "You are worshipped here. You are adored here. You are respected here. We make sacrifices to you here. And for what? What do we get in return for fearing your anger? Look at Dido. She came here, and she got at little price land on which to build her city. I proposed marriage to her; she turned me down. Instead, she is having an adulterous love affair with Aeneas, a womanizer like Paris, who ran away with Helen and started the Trojan War. Aeneas' Trojans are like eunuchs. Aeneas prettifies himself with oiled hair and with effeminate clothing. He gets Dido and Carthage, and we get nothing although we keep sacrificing to you. This is not fair."

Jupiter heard the prayer of Iarbas and so became aware of Aeneas' actions. Jupiter now paid attention to Carthage and to the adulterous love affair of Aeneas and Dido.

Jupiter ordered Mercury to come to him. He then gave Mercury orders to take to Aeneas: "Tell him that he is ignoring his destiny. He should not be in Carthage. He should be working to found his own city. This is not why his mother, Venus, saved him from the attack by Diomedes against him in the Trojan War. This is not why his mother saved him during the fall of Troy. Carthage is not his destiny.

"Italy is his destiny. He must go there and fight a war and establish a city and the Roman people. He must found a people who will bring law to the entire world.

"If Aeneas is not concerned about his own destiny, he ought to be concerned about the destiny of his son. Unless Aeneas goes to Italy, Ascanius will not have a glorious future. Ascanius is also supposed to have Italian offspring. His blood is also supposed to flow in the veins of Romans.

"Aeneas must not stay in Carthage: He must go to Italy. Give him this message from me: You must set sail!"

Mercury put on the winged golden sandals that sped him to his destinations. He grabbed the wand that can make ghosts exit the Land of the Dead or enter the Land of the Dead. Mercury's wand can also make men close their eyes in sleep or open their eyes in death.

Mercury flew through the air, and he saw Atlas, a Titan who used to hold up the sky, and who was transformed into north Africa's Mount Atlas, which holds up the sky. Clouds always surround the crown of Mount Atlas, ice is always in his beard, and snow always covers his shoulders.

Mercury landed on Mount Atlas first, and then he plunged down to the sea the way that a hawk flies above the water and hunts fish. Mercury flew in between the sky and the earth and went to Libya.

Landing at Carthage, Mercury immediately saw Aeneas, who had taken over the duties of Dido and was supervising the building of the city that in years to come would be Rome's greatest enemy. Dressed as a Carthaginian, Aeneas built the walls that Rome would fight against in three wars before finally destroying Carthage as a power in the Mediterranean.

Mercury scorned Aeneas: "Look at what you are doing! You are building the walls of a city that is not your own. You are sleeping with a woman who is your 'wife.' You are ignoring your fate, your destiny. Jupiter ordered me to come here and try to make you sane again. He wants you to stop ignoring your destiny. He wants you to leave Carthage — if not for your own destiny, then for the destiny of your son. Ascanius' destiny lies in Italy, not in Carthage. You owe him the land on which Rome will be built!"

Mercury vanished from Aeneas' sight.

Aeneas had clearly seen and clearly heard Mercury. The god had spoken clearly. Such direct messages from the gods are not to be ignored.

Instantly, Aeneas remembered his duty. He longed to go to Italy. He longed to leave Carthage, although this is a land he loves. He knew that he must obey the commands of Jupiter.

But what about Dido? What can he say to the queen that will have good consequences? How can he break up with a woman who loves him so? What should he do?

Aeneas gave orders to Mnestheus, Sergestus, and Serestus: "Get our ships ready to sail, but tell no one. Make sure that the Trojans are ready to sail. Keep everything secret from the Carthaginians."

Aeneas did not want to leave Dido without saying goodbye, but he did want to wait for a good time to talk to her. He hoped that time would quickly arrive.

Mnestheus, Sergestus, and Serestus quickly followed Aeneas' orders.

But the queen soon heard of a trick, a plot — the Trojans are planning to sail away in secret. She will be left behind without an explanation. Rumor was active, vicious, and destructive. Dido heard rumors that the Trojans were preparing their ships so that they could quickly sail away from Carthage.

Dido was like a Maenad, a wild follower of Bacchus, driven to frenzy by her worship of the god.

Dido spoke to Aeneas before he could speak to her and explain his actions: "Did you really think that you could keep your departure a secret from me? Why do you want to sneak away without even talking to me? Doesn't our love mean anything to you? Would my death mean anything to you?

"Why are you planning to leave now, in winter, a dangerous time to sail? Why would anyone attempt to set sail at this time when the sea is such a danger? The reason for your departure at this time must be me — you are running away because of me!

"Don't I deserve better from you? Aren't we married? Doesn't that mean anything to you? Don't my tears have any effect on you at all?

"If I in fact deserve better than this from you, stay here in Carthage!

"Because of my relationship to you, the tribes and kings that surround Carthage hate me — they are my enemies! Even the Carthaginians hate me because of my relationship with you!

"Because I so much wanted to have a relationship with you, I have broken my vow, I have lost my honor, I have lost my reputation.

"I thought that you would be my permanent husband, but apparently you are my temporary guest.

"What will happen to me now? Will Pygmalion, my brother, the King of Tyre, fight me and conquer the city of Carthage? Will Iarbas force me to become his sex-slave?

"I wish that you had made me pregnant. I wish that I could have your son. I wish that I could have a little Aeneas when you leave — at least, I could look at him and see your features in his face.

"If I could only give birth to your son, I would not feel so abandoned by you."

Dido stopped speaking, and Aeneas resolved to restrain his emotions as he replied to her. Jupiter had reminded him of his destiny and of the destiny of his son, and he thought it best to make a clean break with Dido and not give her a false hope.

Aeneas said, "You have been kind to my Trojans and me. I know this, and the gods know this. I shall always be thankful to you, and I shall always remember you throughout my life. I know that you deserve good things.

"Please let me say a few things.

"I never intended to leave you without saying goodbye. I did not ever intend to sail away from you in secret. Please do not believe that I ever intended such things.

"Also, remember that I am not your husband. We are not legally married. I have never held the torch of a bridegroom, and I have never said the vows of a bridegroom to you.

"If the Fates would have allowed me anything I wished for after the fall of Troy, I would not have come to Carthage. I would have stayed at Troy, and I would have rebuilt the city on its old site. I would have rebuilt the palace of Priam, and I would have rebuilt the fortifications of Troy to keep its defeated citizens safe.

"But I was not allowed to rebuild Troy. The oracle of Apollo at the city of Gyrnia has stated my task, my destiny. I must go to Italy. That will be my new homeland, not Carthage.

"You, yourself, left Tyre and founded a new city — Carthage — in north Africa. I have left Troy and will found a new city in Italy. I want to do what you have done. If what you have done is the right thing to do, we Trojans should not be criticized for wanting to do the same thing.

"My father, Anchises, died in Sicily, but his ghost appears to me in dreams. He warns about things I ought not to do. I fear that I will do what I ought not to do: ignore my destiny.

"I think about my son, Ascanius. He, too, has a destiny. I must fulfill my destiny so that he can fulfill his destiny. I must not rob him of his future kingdom in Italy. Fate has decreed that his kingdom lies there, not in north Africa.

"I swear that a messenger of the gods who was sent by Jupiter appeared before me and brought me the commands of Jupiter himself. I saw and heard clearly Jupiter's messenger. He ordered me to achieve my destiny.

"Do not try to prevent me from sailing. You will be hurting both of us with your futile attempts.

"Yes, I will set sail for Italy — by the order of Jupiter, not of my own free will."

As Aeneas had spoken to her, Dido had glared at him. She had looked him over, as she silently stood. Now she shrieked at him, "Venus is not your mother! Dardanus is not your ancestor! Your parents are not immortal gods or mortal humans! Mount Caucasus with its rocks must be your father! The tigers of Hyrcania must have suckled you!

"How do I know this? Because you have no pity for me. Did you groan as you spoke to me? No. Did you even look at me? No. Did you cry as you ought to have done? No. Why do you not pity me — I love you!

"Why aren't Jupiter and Juno helping me? Why aren't they taking pity on me? Shouldn't the gods have a sense of fairness?

"You washed up on the shores of Carthage, and I gave you food, clothing, and shelter. I let you rule my kingdom. I saved your ships, and I saved your Trojans.

"The Furies are the gods who concern themselves with me. They madden me.

"The gods who concern themselves with you are Apollo and his oracles. They tell you what to do. So does Jupiter, who sends a messenger with orders for you. This is work for gods? Don't they have better things to do?

"So go to Italy. I won't stop you.

"But I hope that the gods do. I hope that you and your ships are wrecked on rocks in the middle of the sea. I hope that you die while crying out my name again and again. While I am alive, I will wish only evil for you.

"After I die, my ghost will follow you wherever you go. After I am dead, I will wish only evil for you. I will haunt you.

"Even when I am in the Land of the Dead, I will wish only evil for you. News of you will reach me even there, and bad news about you will comfort me."

Dido ran away from Aeneas, leaving him behind, unhappy. Once out of the room, she fainted and her serving women caught her and took her to her chamber and placed her on her bed.

Aeneas now pursued his duty. He felt bad about Dido, but he knew that he must pursue his destiny. Instead of going to Dido and talking to her, he went to his ships and worked to make them seaworthy.

He and his men worked hard. They brought timber with which to repair the ships and to make oars. They worked as hard as ants when they find a huge mound of wheat and pillage it and take it to their home. Some ants carry the grains of wheat, and some ants supervise the workers and punish the lazy. The Trojans repaired their ships and put them back in the water.

Dido witnessed the Trojans' labor. She looked out at all of the activity on the beach and mourned. Her lover was getting ready to leave her.

Love can be a cruel tyrant. It often treats people badly. Dido cried. She wanted Aeneas back. She tried to think of ways to get him back.

Dido said to Anna, her sister, "Look at the Trojan ships in the water. They are nearly ready to sail. I know that Aeneas wants to leave me, but go to him. You know him; he and you have been friends. Plead with him. Remind him that my ships did not join the Greek ships at Aulis where they sacrificed Agamemnon's daughter Iphigenia before sailing across the sea to attack Troy. Remind him that I never made a vow to make war against Troy. Remind him that I never sent ships to attack Troy. I have done nothing that would ever hurt his father, Anchises, either while Anchises was alive or after his death.

"Why should Aeneas be in such a hurry to leave? Make a request of him for me: Ask him to wait a while longer so that he will have safe sailing weather. He will need good winds and a smooth sea.

"I no longer request that he observe our marriage. I don't expect him to forget his destiny that lies in Latium.

"I do ask him to give me time — time to partially recover from the loss of his love.

"If he will give me time now, I will pay him back more than I owe when I die."

So Dido pleaded to her sister, who spoke to Aeneas and told him of Dido's tears. But Dido's tears did not turn Aeneas from his destiny. Fate had decreed that he go to Italy.

A huge tree can be blasted by the North wind, which tries to uproot it. The tree limbs move, but the tree stays firmly rooted. Aeneas was like that tree. He heard the appeals that Anna made, but he stayed true to his destiny.

Tears fell. In vain.

Consumed by *furor*, Dido resolved to die. She was tired of living. She laid gifts for the gods on an altar, and the omens were terrifying. She put holy water on the altar — the water turned black. She poured out wine for the gods — the wine turned to blood. She did not tell anyone — not even her sister — about the omens.

She went at night to a marble temple that held a shrine dedicated to her late husband: Sychaeus. She seemed to hear his voice calling her name from the Land of the Dead.

She heard an owl on a rooftop calling out what appeared to be a lament for the dead: a dirge.

She remembered the prophecies of seers of ancient times. The prophecies were terrifying, and they made her afraid.

She had nightmares about Aeneas: He was a savage hunter who wanted to kill her.

She had other nightmares: She wandered alone, looking for her people in a strange country.

She felt like Pentheus, who was driven insane by Bacchus because he did not respect the god. In his manic *furor*, his vision became double, and he saw two suns when only one existed, and he saw two cities of Thebes when only one existed.

She felt like Orestes, the son of Agamemnon. Consumed by *furor*, Orestes killed his mother, and so the Furies pursued him, driving him mad — he saw his dead mother threatening him with fire and snakes and he tried to run from her, but the Furies blocked his way.

Maddened with *furor*, Dido thought about her death. How should she die? When should she die?

Dido went to her sister, and putting on an act so Anna would not know what she was planning, she spoke to Anna calmly, "I have good news. I have found a way to do one of two things: make Aeneas love me again, or make me forget my love for him. In Ethiopia is a priestess who takes care of the temple of the daughters of the Evening Star. She takes care of the sacred grove, and she feeds honey and poppies to the dragon. The priestess knows spells for various purposes: how to end passionate love, how to cause pain, how to stop a river, how to make stars cross the sky in a different direction, how to bring the dead out of Hades, and how to cause an earthquake. She knows magic, and although I am reluctant to do it, I will use her magic now.

"Please do as I ask you. Build a funeral pyre in the inner courtyard in the open air. Don't let people know what you are doing. On the funeral pyre, put Aeneas' armor and weapons. He left them in our bedroom; he has not taken them. On the funeral pyre, put Aeneas' clothing and put the bed he and I slept in. The funeral pyre will burn every trace of Aeneas that remains in Carthage. So works the priestess' spell."

Dido fell silent, and her face grew pale.

Anna suspected nothing. She did not know that her sister was planning to commit suicide. She felt that Dido would grieve for Aeneas only as much she had grieved for her late husband.

But the queen took action when the funeral pyre was built under the sky in the inner courtyard. She placed funeral wreathes in her palace. She put an effigy of Aeneas on the bed on the funeral pyre, beside his armor and his sword.

Dido then performed rites of magic. At the altars by the funeral pyre, with her hair and robes unbound, in accordance with the rites of magic, she named three hundred gods, including Erebus, Chaos, and Hecate, goddess of the Land of the Dead, who was also Diana, a goddess huntress on earth, and Luna, the goddess of the moon.

Dido sprinkled water that represented the waters found in Hell. She found poisonous herbs by the light of the moon. She used the membrane that had covered a colt when it was born. With only one foot wearing a sandal, in accordance with the rites of magic, she prayed to gods who knew that she was about to commit suicide. She also prayed to any god — should one exist — who cares for lovers who love each other unequally, with only one lover greatly loving the other.

It was night, and everything and everyone but Dido was at rest. The woods were calm, the sea was calm, and the stars moved in their usual course.

Dido could not sleep; she could not stop thinking about her love for Aeneas and his refusal of her love.

She said to herself, "What should I do? What are my options? I have rejected proposals of marriage here in Libya. Should I make a fool of myself and urge kings to propose to me again?

"Or should I follow the Trojans as they sail away? I have helped them — oh, so recently — but will they remember? Will they welcome me? More likely, they will hate me. Haven't I realized yet that the Trojans are as untrustworthy as their early king, Laomedon, who cheated Poseidon and Apollo after they had worked for him for a year at the command of Jupiter? Haven't I realized yet that the Trojans are as untrustworthy as their early king, Laomedon, who tried to cheat Hercules of the horses that he had promised him after Hercules had rescued Laomedon's daughter?

"Should I follow Trojan ships by myself? Or should I follow Trojan ships with all my Carthaginians? Would my Carthaginians be willing to leave their new city? No. I found it hard enough to get them to leave Tyre and sail to north Africa. I will not be able to uproot them again.

"Therefore, it is best that I die.

"I deserve to die.

"I will end my life with the sword of Aeneas.

"I cried in front of Anna, and she advised me to seek love. She advised me to do what would be best for my new city. I gave in to her and to my love, and this is the result. Much better it would have been never to have felt love again, never to have been tempted to be married, never to have been tempted to break the vow I made to myself and the ashes of my late husband. I broke that vow!"

Dido agonized that night; Aeneas slept peacefully on one of his ships.

Mercury appeared to Aeneas in a dream. The blond god said to him, "Why are you asleep? Why aren't you sailing? The West wind is blowing, ready to take you away from Carthage.

"Dido, who is unhappy, is thinking about treachery, so leave now.

"Set sail now, while you still can. If you don't set sail now, tomorrow you will see your ships set on fire.

"Worry about your destiny, not about a woman. Women change; your destiny is unchanging."

Aeneas woke up. He took action, waking up his men and ordering them to set sail: "I have seen a god. He wants us to set sail — now!" He prayed to the god, "We will do as you say. Help us. Give us good sailing weather."

Aeneas used his sword to cut the rope that moored his ship. The crews of the other ships did the same. Soon, the harbor was empty of Trojan ships; they were at sea.

Dawn arrived, and Dido looked out at the harbor from her high tower. It was empty of Trojan ships, and she mourned. She beat her breasts and tore her hair in the ancient way of showing grief.

Dido lamented, "This stranger — Aeneas — has mocked Carthage. We Carthaginians should arm ourselves, set sail in our ships, and overtake the Trojans! We can fight the Trojans with weapons! We can set their ships on fire in the sea!

"But no. I am not making sense. I have already resolved to die.

"I am unhappy now, and I have been unhappy. I have acted the wrong way.

"Aeneas is supposed to be a good man. He carried his father out of burning Troy! He carried his household gods out of burning Troy! But is Aeneas a good man?

"I should have killed Aeneas when I first saw him. I should have killed his men. I should have killed Aeneas' son, cooked him, and served him to Aeneas.

"We Carthaginians should have fought a battle with the Trojans. The victory might have gone to the Trojans, but so what? Either way, win or lose, I, Dido, would have died. I should have set their camp on fire and burned their ships. I should have killed both Aeneas and Ascanius and then myself!

"Hear my prayers, sun, Juno, underworld goddess Hecate, and avenging Furies! Listen to me. I deserve that much. If Aeneas is fated to fulfill his destiny and found his city in Latium, let him and his descendants suffer from my curse! Let him fight a war in Italy. Let him beg for help and see his people die. Let him have a peace that is not just, that lacks *clementia*. Let him not enjoy his unjust peace. Let him die early. Let him lie unburied.

"I pray this with my words and with my blood. I also pray that my Carthaginians will forever be the enemies of his descendants. Let the Carthaginians' hatred for Aeneas' descendants be an offering made to my ghost. May the Carthaginians and Aeneas' descendants never love each other and never be at peace.

"I pray that a Carthaginian avenger, now unknown, will rise up in the future and battle the descendants of Aeneas. I curse Aeneas' descendants with war — unending war!"

Maddened by *furor*, Dido then turned her thoughts to suicide.

To Barce, the nurse of her late husband — her own nurse had died in Tyre — Dido said, "Ask Anna to come to me. Anna must sprinkle herself with river water in preparation for a sacrifice. She must bring the sacrificial animals here. You and she must wear the sacred headbands for the sacrifice. I am ready to set the rite in motion. I will end my love for Aeneas."

Barce set off on her errand.

Dido was frenzied by *furor*. Her eyes rolled, and her face paled. She climbed the funeral pyre and unsheathed a Trojan sword. The sword was a gift, but the giver had not intended that it be used for this purpose.

She looked at Aeneas' clothing and the bed that they had slept in. She wept, and she lay down on the funeral pyre and said her last words: "I am ready to die. I am ready to end my suffering. I am ready to be free of pain. I have lived my life. I have lived what I have been fated to live. I am ready to journey to the Land of the Dead. I have built a great city. I have avenged the death of my husband and punished my brother, who murdered my husband. I have been happy, and I would have continued to be happy if only the Trojans had not landed here."

Dido pressed her face into the bed that she had shared with Aeneas, and then she said, "I will die without a present avenger. So be it. I will die willingly, and I will make my way to the Land of the Dead. I much prefer that to continuing to live. I hope that Aeneas sees the smoke of my funeral pyre far out at sea. Let it be a bad omen for him."

Maddened by *furor*, Dido fell on the sword. Blood reddened the sword; blood reddened her hands. Female servants screamed.

Rumor ran like a maddened follower of Bacchus throughout Carthage. The Carthaginians mourned; the women cried and shrieked. It sounded as if a city — Tyre or Carthage — were falling to enemy soldiers, and waves of fire were destroying the city.

Anna heard the cries of grief and despair. Terrified, and mourning, she scratched her face and beat her breasts and cried, "Dido, is this what you wanted? Is this why you wanted the funeral pyre? You have deceived me. You have hurt me. You should have told me what you planned to do — we could have died together. I built this funeral pyre at your request. I did not know what you planned to do. You have destroyed so much: your life, my life, and your people and city.

"Come, women of Carthage, and help me to bathe my sister's wounds. Let me be with my sister in her final moments of life."

Anna climbed to the top of the funeral pyre and held her dying sister in her arms. Anna cried. She used her gown to try to stop Dido's bleeding.

The wound had penetrated one of Dido's lungs. As she labored to breathe, her wound hissed.

Three times Dido tried to raise herself on one of her elbows. Three times she failed.

Dido looked at the sky and sought the sun. When she saw it, it hurt her eyes and she moaned.

Dido was dying hard.

Juno saw her and pitied her. Dido was dying at the wrong time, too early a time. Because Dido's death was a suicide, Proserpina, the Queen of the Land of the Dead, refused to come and cut the lock of hair that would free Dido from life and from an agonizing death. Juno sent Iris down to free Dido. Iris flew to Dido, held a lock of her hair, and said, "As commanded by Juno, I cut this lock of hair — an offering to the god of Death — and I release you from life and from your body."

Iris cut the lock of hair, and the warmth left Dido's body and her breath fled with the wind.

NOTE: This is an excerpt from David Bruce's book *Virgil's* Aeneid: *A Retelling in Prose.*

APPENDIX B: ABOUT THE AUTHOR

It was a dark and stormy night. Suddenly a cry rang out, and on a hot summer night in 1954, Josephine, wife of Carl Bruce, gave birth to a boy — me. Unfortunately, this young married couple allowed Reuben Saturday, Josephine's brother, to name their first-born. Reuben, aka "The Joker," decided that Bruce was a nice name, so he decided to name me Bruce Bruce. I have gone by my middle name — David — ever since.

Being named Bruce David Bruce hasn't been all bad. Bank tellers remember me very quickly, so I don't often have to show an ID. It can be fun in charades, also. When I was a counselor as a teenager at Camp Echoing Hills in Warsaw, Ohio, a fellow counselor gave the signs for "sounds like" and "two words," then she pointed to a bruise on her leg twice. Bruise Bruise? Oh yeah, Bruce Bruce is the answer!

Uncle Reuben, by the way, gave me a haircut when I was in kindergarten. He cut my hair short and shaved a small bald spot on the back of my head. My mother wouldn't let me go to school until the bald spot grew out again.

Of all my brothers and sisters (six in all), I am the only transplant to Athens, Ohio. I was born in Newark, Ohio, and have lived all around Southeastern Ohio. However, I moved to Athens to go to Ohio University and have never left.

At Ohio U, I never could make up my mind whether to major in English or Philosophy, so I got a bachelor's degree with a double major in both areas, then I added a Master of Arts degree in English and a Master of Arts degree in Philosophy. Yes, I have my MAMA degree.

Currently, and for a long time to come (I eat fruits and veggies), I am spending my retirement writing books such as *Nadia Comaneci: Perfect 10*, *The Funniest People in Dance*, *Homer's* Iliad: *A Retelling in Prose*, and *William Shakespeare's* Othello: *A Retelling in Prose*.

By the way, my sister Brenda Kennedy writes romances such as *A New Beginning* and *Shattered Dreams*.

By the way, my sister Brenda Kennedy writes romances such as *A New Beginning* and *Shattered Dreams*.

APPENDIX C: SOME BOOKS BY DAVID BRUCE

Retellings of a Classic Work of Literature

Arden of Faversham: *A Retelling*

Ben Jonson's The Alchemist: *A Retelling*

Ben Jonson's The Arraignment, or Poetaster: *A Retelling*

Ben Jonson's Bartholomew Fair: *A Retelling*

Ben Jonson's The Case is Altered: *A Retelling*

Ben Jonson's Catiline's Conspiracy: *A Retelling*

Ben Jonson's The Devil is an Ass: *A Retelling*

Ben Jonson's Epicene: *A Retelling*

Ben Jonson's Every Man in His Humor: *A Retelling*

Ben Jonson's Every Man Out of His Humor: *A Retelling*

Ben Jonson's The Fountain of Self-Love, or Cynthia's Revels: *A Retelling*

Ben Jonson's The Magnetic Lady, or Humors Reconciled: *A Retelling*

Ben Jonson's The New Inn, or The Light Heart: *A Retelling*

Ben Jonson's Sejanus' Fall: *A Retelling*

Ben Jonson's The Staple of News: *A Retelling*

Ben Jonson's A Tale of a Tub: *A Retelling*

Ben Jonson's Volpone, or the Fox: *A Retelling*

Christopher Marlowe's Complete Plays: Retellings

Christopher Marlowe's Dido, Queen of Carthage: *A Retelling*

Christopher Marlowe's Doctor Faustus: *Retellings of the 1604 A-Text and of the 1616 B-Text*

Christopher Marlowe's Edward II: *A Retelling*

Christopher Marlowe's The Massacre at Paris: *A Retelling*

Christopher Marlowe's The Rich Jew of Malta: *A Retelling*

Christopher Marlowe's Tamburlaine, Parts 1 and 2: *Retellings*

Dante's Divine Comedy: *A Retelling in Prose*

Dante's Inferno: *A Retelling in Prose*

Dante's Purgatory: *A Retelling in Prose*

Dante's Paradise: *A Retelling in Prose*

The Famous Victories of Henry V: *A Retelling*

From the Iliad *to the* Odyssey: *A Retelling in Prose of Quintus of Smyrna's* Posthomerica

George Chapman, Ben Jonson, and John Marston's Eastward Ho! *A Retelling*

George Peele's The Arraignment of Paris: *A Retelling*

George Peele's The Battle of Alcazar: *A Retelling*

George Peele's David and Bathsheba, and the Tragedy of Absalom: *A Retelling*

George Peele's Edward I: *A Retelling*

George Peele's The Old Wives' Tale: *A Retelling*

George-a-Greene: *A Retelling*

The History of King Leir: *A Retelling*

Homer's Iliad: *A Retelling in Prose*

Homer's Odyssey: *A Retelling in Prose*

J.W. Gent.'s The Valiant Scot: *A Retelling*

Jason and the Argonauts: A Retelling in Prose of Apollonius of Rhodes' Argonautica

John Ford: Eight Plays Translated into Modern English

John Ford's The Broken Heart: *A Retelling*

John Ford's The Fancies, Chaste and Noble: *A Retelling*

John Ford's The Lady's Trial: *A Retelling*

John Ford's The Lover's Melancholy: *A Retelling*

John Ford's Love's Sacrifice: *A Retelling*

John Ford's Perkin Warbeck: *A Retelling*

John Ford's The Queen: *A Retelling*

John Ford's 'Tis Pity She's a Whore: *A Retelling*

John Lyly's Campaspe: *A Retelling*

John Lyly's Endymion, The Man in the Moon: *A Retelling*

John Lyly's Galatea: *A Retelling*

John Lyly's Love's Metamorphosis: *A Retelling*

John Lyly's Midas: *A Retelling*

John Lyly's Mother Bombie: *A Retelling*

John Lyly's Sappho and Phao: *A Retelling*

John Lyly's The Woman in the Moon: *A Retelling*

John Webster's The White Devil: *A Retelling*

King Edward III: *A Retelling*

Mankind: *A Medieval Morality Play* (A Retelling)

Margaret Cavendish's The Unnatural Tragedy: *A Retelling*

The Merry Devil of Edmonton: *A Retelling*

The Summoning of Everyman: *A Medieval Morality Play* (A Retelling)

Robert Greene's Friar Bacon and Friar Bungay: *A Retelling*

The Taming of a Shrew: *A Retelling*

Tarlton's Jests: A Retelling

Thomas Middleton's A Chaste Maid in Cheapside: *A Retelling*

Thomas Middleton's Women Beware Women: *A Retelling*

www.ingramcontent.com/pod-product-compliance
Lightning Source LLC
Chambersburg PA
CBHW031437150726
47989CB00002B/973